# "I am offering you my name and my protection."

Marcus's voice did not betray any emotion.

Too shocked at the notion to guard her expression, Catherine's lips parted in astonishment. "You can't be serious!"

He nodded grimly. "Oh, but I am. Despite this—" he fingered the scar on his cheek "—I am still a man, and I wish to start my family, have a wife to grace my table and stand at my side."

"But you don't know me. I have nothing to bring to you," she reminded him.

"Excuses. I guess your need was not as great as I thought," he said bitterly.

"I'll marry you," Catherine said quickly, lest he change his mind.

Marcus simply nodded. "So be it," he declared, and left the room.

Catherine, full of wonder, gazed into the fire. Her future had a silver lining after all. She would be safe with a dream she had never expected to come true. She had no illusions, but she would make this misfit match work. If it were within her power, Marcus would

# MISFIT MATCH

## SYDNEY ANN CLARY

**Harlequin Books**

TORONTO • NEW YORK • LONDON
AMSTERDAM • PARIS • SYDNEY • HAMBURG
STOCKHOLM • ATHENS • TOKYO • MILAN

Published November 1989

ISBN 0-373-31113-3

# PROLOGUE

THE STEADY THUNDER of heavy cannons rent the powder-laden air as horse and rider picked their way up the hill where another horseman waited. The motionless figure on the promontory appeared unaware of the man's approach, his gaze concentrated on the battle raging below. As far as could be seen, the scarlet coats of the English troops were engaged with Napoleon's rabble horde, both sides neither giving nor asking any quarter. The clash of steel on steel, the screams of wounded horses, all mixed with the battle cries to produce a din as deafening as it was awe inspiring.

Marcus, the Earl of Barrington, drew his tired mare to a halt beside the Duke of Wellington's white stallion, his eyes, too, trained on the carnage below.

The members of the London scene would have found it difficult to recognize their favoured star, so changed was he from the beautifully attired gentleman Sally Jersey once described as the epitome of a modern-day Adonis. The thick hair, which then gleamed black as a raven's wing, was dull and liberally covered in ash and the dust of countless miles.

The classic Greek features responsible for more than one young girl's swoon were deeply etched with fatigue and worry. His slender frame was honed to rapier-like sharpness, strength evident in the way he sat straight in the saddle after twenty-four hours, ferrying vital battle directives between Wellington and his subordinates.

"The left flank isn't holding up as I hoped, Marcus," the duke observed, drawing his aide's attention to the ragged retreat of the outnumbered English squadron before the furious onslaught of the French. "Get a fresh horse and see what you can do. It is imperative they hold, or all we have gained will be lost."

Grasping the urgency of the situation, Marcus kicked his jaded mount into an unsteady trot down the hill toward the rear lines and a fresh horse. This was not the first time he had been ordered on such a mission. On each occasion he had successfully carried out his instructions.

Minutes later Marcus dodged flailing hooves as he leapt lightly astride the nervous gelding of Sir Harry Stanton's. Precious seconds were lost while he fought the terrified horse to bring him under control. Finally his mount stood relatively quiet as the head groom tightened the girth.

"Sorry, m'lord, I ain't got no better. Hardly fit he is, I know, being as Sir Harry, rest his soul, never used him but for huntin'," the man said apologetically, giving the bay a final pat.

"Thanks, Sam. See to the mare for me. She's earned a rest," the earl said before wheeling around and departing at a brisk canter.

The horse moved readily at his command although the noise was not to his liking. Marcus's arms ached from the constant pull on the reins. He hung on with grim purpose, picking his way through the maze of fallen trees, cannon holes and wounded comrades. The closer he drew to his destination, the louder the din grew. His nose and eyes burned from the thick haze of powder, dirt and smoke. Ahead, seeing the enemy engaged in hand-to-hand struggle, he drew his sword and charged into the fray shouting encouragement to the lagging men.

The fresh cry of strength and assurance steadied the ragged line. Exhaustion ebbed as red-rimmed eyes focused on the slender figure atop the wheeling, screaming bay. Each swish of his gleaming blade radiated fresh hope. Gaps closed, the line of scarlet coats tightened and finally held. Slowly, ever so slowly, the tide turned. Inches of precious ground became feet and feet became yards. The French fell back with increasing speed before the growing fury of the inspired English.

Marcus was an easy target among the infantry. Suddenly, out of the billowing clouds, emerged a huge war horse carrying a massive rider. The grey bore down on his slighter foe in lumbering strides. Marcus's sword swung, dropping his opponent just as the shadow of the approaching enemy loomed over him. He scarcely had time to bring up his blade to deflect the sabre descending toward his heart.

Pain shot through his arm as steel met steel, his sword breaking beneath the strain. The bay went to his knees, throwing Marcus completely off balance and saving his life in the bargain. Instead of finding its target, the French blade slashed jaggedly down Marcus's left cheek and across his shoulder.

Intent on remaining astride and in control of his mount despite the fact that his left arm now hung useless at his side, the earl was scarcely aware of the injury to his face. One-handed, he had little say in the direction the crazed horse took. All he knew was suddenly he was free of the deadly tangle, and before his fast blurring eyes stretched the safety of the rear lines. Then darkness closed in around him as he slumped, unconscious, against the gelding's neck. His last conscious action was to tighten his grip on the reins and grab a handful of red mane.

MARCUS PROWLED THE CONFINES of his tent, flexing his injured shoulder with each step. Four weeks, and still he was not fit for duty. Fever had overcome him those first two weeks, leaving him weak as a sick cat. Dreams. Only the dreams of Lady Barbara had kept him calm as Bates had alternately nursed and clucked over him as a hen with one chick.

Lady Barbara Carr! The reigning belle of the season. His, all his, or at least she soon would be when this cursed war was won. With all of London at her dainty feet, he had sought and won her hand in marriage. The pride he felt at their betrothal ball flooded his thoughts as the vivid image of her beauty returned to enchant him. Poised on the stairs like a delicate golden bird, she was the epitome of English womanhood. Sapphire-blue eyes sparkling with success and pleasure shone more radiantly than the Barrington diamonds around her lovely neck. Her golden hair gleamed beneath the candles with such brilliance anyone could have been forgiven for gasping aloud.

When her slender hand rested on his arm as they were congratulated by their friends, he knew his world to be complete. He had found an angel to rival even his beloved mother. With Lady Barbara by his side, he, too, would know the happiness his parents had had in such full measure.

The Perfect Couple! How right that *on dit* was. Barbara was all he hoped for and more. Her pretty helplessness made him ache to protect her from the harshness of the world. Her pleasure at the presents he bestowed upon her delighted him. She never failed to show off her treasures to her friends, something which caused him to suffer many a sly comment on his lavish generosity. Of course, the sky-blue phaeton drawn by the elegant white mare was a bit more than a little trinket, but he really could not resist the plea on her rosy lips and the dew-drenched look in her eyes when he had suggested she wait until they were married. How he missed Barbara and longed to be at her side. But first he had his duty to complete....

The sound of footsteps outside the tent drew his attention. He turned to face the opening of the flap.

"Good morning, my lord. You wished to see me." The duke's private physician paused, his eyes surveying his patient critically.

"I did. It has been four weeks now," Marcus announced, dispensing with courtesy for once. "I want to know when I may be up and about my business."

The doctor eyed him carefully. "May I be seated first?" he asked.

The earl nodded, his glance following him to the rough stool beside his own chair. "Well?" he prompted.

"What do you wish to know?"

Marcus's temper exploded at the calm, almost indifferent question. "Hell's teeth! What do you think I wish to know? What the weather is?" he demanded angrily. "When shall I return to my post?"

"You will not," the physician answered baldly.

"Why? What is it you and Bates aren't telling me?" He studied the man intently. Comprehension came as the silence lengthened. "That's why it is taking so long to heal," he observed slowly. "It will not."

The doctor shook his head. "I fear not. The wound itself will eventually, but your arm will always be stiff. The injury to the shoulder was too deep. You were fortunate to keep your arm at all.''

Marcus scowled. This he had not foreseen. The ultimate irony. When most of his contemporaries had damned him for a fool for volunteering to fight the French, he had known he owed it to his country to serve. And now he was being denied the opportunity. ''Fortunate? Is that how you view it?''

''Yes, damn it, I do. So your face is no longer handsome,'' he began.

''As if I cared about that. It's my arm that matters,'' he argued, incensed.

''At least you have two,'' the other man almost shouted. ''Some aren't so blessed. I have just come from surgery on a boy who lost both his legs. He has no wealth to cushion his way, no family to care that he will never walk again.''

The earl took the facer without blinking. He had deserved the setdown. He knew well there were many far worse off than he. Slowly common sense asserted itself. Resignation replaced his anger. He could not remain. So be it. There was still London and Barbara. Her love was a beacon shining in the darkness of his despair. Although he was no longer fit for active service, perhaps there was still something he could do when he returned home. He looked up to find the doctor watching him, sympathy and compassion in his eyes.

"Thank you," he said simply.

The physician took his acceptance with relief. Odd how little his facial scar appeared to bother the earl, he thought as he rose to leave. Somehow he would have believed otherwise.

# CHAPTER ONE

CATHERINE SHEPHERDED her charges into the morning room, seeing to it that Victoria and Melissa were seated properly and in full view of their mother—Catherine's aunt, Lady Carr. Only then did she take her own place in the straight-backed chair in the far corner. Folding her hands neatly in her lap, she prepared herself for the ritual of taking tea with her family. Not that she would be offered any of the refreshment. No, her only role was that of governess, and oft times servant. Being an impoverished cousin thrown onto the charity of Lady Carr had been an unexpected upheaval in her young life. Having never known the pleasure of wealth she had not missed it. What she did miss was the kindness and love that had always abounded in her own home. Glancing down at her hands, she tried to put the past from her mind. What could not be changed had to be endured. Her father and her mother had believed that. She must, as well.

"Barbara, you cannot possibly be serious!" Lady Carr's angry voice echoed in the elegant morning room. She paid scant heed to the two youngest of her offspring and their cousin-cum-governess, Catherine. Her whole attention was concentrated on the other female in the room, her oldest daughter. "How could you? What Lord Barrington will say if he gets wind of this I cannot think."

The object of her displeasure shrugged a dainty, velvet-clad shoulder, her beautiful face marred by an expression of petulance. "Oh, Mama, it is beyond anything reasonable to expect me to moulder away in this great barn all year. It is bad enough that we must pretend we *chose* to stay in London instead of repairing to Bath as have the rest of our friends. And you tell me I cannot do this or cannot do that because of what people will say. Stuff! Why, Marcus would be the first one to agree I must be permitted my pleasures. He is not so Gothic, I assure you!"

"Mind your impertinence, my girl! Do you believe he will countenance your making a byword of yourself with Lord March while he serves his country? Have a care what you're about for all our sakes. Your folly could well whistle his wealth down the wind, and then what, pray? You cannot be such a fool as to believe Lord March means marriage. Although his background is unexceptional despite that French grandmother of his, he is a known flirt."

Lady Carr's bosom heaved with the force of her emotions. Clearly she had forgotten the presence of the three younger listeners. Though she doted on Barbara and revelled in her extraordinary beauty and success with the ton, she was mercenary to a fault.

She meant to do her all to prevent her daughter's indiscreet behaviour from destroying one of the most brilliant matches of the season.

Judging from the mulish expression on her Barbara's face, she was losing the battle. Drat the chit! She knew well how important the Barrington wealth was to the disgustingly empty Carr family coffers. Setting aside the marriage settlement, which was some setting aside considering the enormous size of it, there were still Melissa and Victoria to launch. Having a wealthy, well-connected sibling would go a long way in overcoming the shortage of their dowries. Few would turn up their noses at a chance of a kinship by marriage with the house of Barrington. Though all these thoughts flashed like lightning through Lady Carr's head, the harsh set of her face did not change.

Lady Carr had opened her mouth to deliver the lecture Barbara not only needed but richly deserved when her sharp eyes caught the movement of her daughter, Victoria, as she fidgeted in her chair by the window. Fixing the hapless twelve-year-old with an angry look, she bade her to cease. Turning to her niece, she said, "Really, Catherine, what on earth do I keep you for if not to control two girls? Of all the inept creatures I ever laid eyes on, you are the most impossible."

Catherine looked up, flushing to the roots of her tied-back hair. Worried huge emerald green eyes stared out of a thin, pale face.

"I'm sorry, Aunt, shall I take the children away...?" her soft whisper died away as Catherine observed the effect of her innocent suggestion.

She was well acquainted with her aunt's temper when crossed. She had spoken without being asked. Fatalistically, she waited with bowed head for the strident voice of her aunt to remind her of her ingratitude to the charitable generosity of her relatives. After the first few words, Catherine's mind ceased to register the attack. Instead, she wandered through the corridors and shadows of the past.

The sunlight dappled the early morning with warmth and brightness. The small manor house smelled faintly of beeswax and the pot-pourri her mother placed in each room. Even now she well remembered the sweet odour and the presence of love in the slightly shabby rooms. Echoes of her mother's soft voice and her father's deep, yet gentle answers brought tears to her eyes. So much gone! The results of a young buck's drunken wager. Her parents, her home and the love she knew all in a fatal freak accident on one of their infrequent journeys to London three years ago. Just for a moment she gave in to the grief of the loss of her family. Tiny drops splashed on her tightly clenched hands as her ears caught the shrill echoes of "pity, charity, debt and gratitude."

Her aunt, seeing the evidence of her niece's repentance, was satisfied to leave her victim suitably chastised. Never for a moment did she suspect the real cause of the distress written so plainly on Catherine's face. In the unlikely event Lady Carr had known, she would have condemned Catherine for her stupidity in repining on the past.

Lady Carr switched her attention back to her oldest daughter and returned to the subject at hand with undiminished vigour.

"Now, miss, make no mistake, you will not be driving out with Lord March today or any other day," she stated firmly, never doubting her ability to command her wishes.

"Mama," Barbara wailed in earnest, "never say I can't see Robert. Please reconsider, I beg. He only amuses me, I promise you. Surely there is no harm in that."

"For how long, you fool? You cannot be so green you don't know what he wants. Good Gad, girl, he means no good."

The stalemate between the two equally determined women was broken by a discreet tap on the closed door.

Catherine jumped up to answer the summons. She stepped back to permit the entrance of the butler bearing an impressive-looking letter on a silver tray.

"Don't just stand there, man. What is it?" Lady Carr demanded peevishly, thoroughly disgusted with her entire household. She was surrounded by fools, the woman thought in self-righteous anger.

"'Tis a letter, my lady, from his lordship, the Earl of Barrington," he explained stiffly.

Magically the tense atmosphere in the room dissipated. Lady Carr's unbecoming colour faded, and her frown was replaced by a smile resembling that of a well-fed cat. Catherine glanced at Barbara, disturbed by the almost bored expression on her cousin's face. Until recently the earl's letters had been arriving with great regularity since his departure. Catherine could not help but worry at the strange lapse in communication, although no one else in the house had appeared distressed.

All eyes were fastened on Barbara as she accepted the missive and gracefully sank onto the cream satin settee and arranged her sable-brown skirts around her feet. True to her nature, she revelled in the power of being the centre of interest, and she played her part to the utmost.

"When Lord March calls, please tender my daughter's regrets," Lady Carr directed, dismissing the servant with a flick of her hand before she turned her attention to her daughter.

Although Catherine rarely had cause to agree with her aunt, she found herself doing so now. She, too, had wondered what Barbara was about to encourage so shocking a rake as Lord March. The fact that her aunt saw fit to call her beloved daughter to task before her penniless niece was a measure of her own uncharacteristic anxiety. Catherine waited, scarcely daring to so much as breathe, hoping she and her charges would not be dismissed before the earl's letter was read. Though she was not normally inter-

ested in Barbara's affairs, she thought it important
to know how the earl went on. She had heard whispers of his courage. The gentle man who had de-
parted the city was rumoured to be a lion on the field
of battle.

As the silence lengthened, broken only by the slow
turning of the pages of the earl's letter, Catherine
recalled vividly the image of ebony eyes alight with
admiration for Barbara's beauty. Strange, she could
remember the earl's features in such detail when she
had caught only occasional, short glimpses of him.
What with between controlling her two curious
charges and other duties, she scarce had time for
more than quick glances whenever the earl had arrived to take her cousin out driving or to an evening
engagement.

One night stood out in Catherine's mind. It was
Barbara's betrothal ball and she had been beautiful
as usual. And for once she had managed to be on
time, an almost unheard-of circumstance. It had
hardly seemed fair to deny her young sisters a
glimpse of the joys awaiting them. True, they had
barely escaped detection in their hiding place among
the shadows of the upper landing.

For a moment Catherine allowed her imagination
to take over. Barbara's image disappeared and in her
place it was she, Catherine, who stood exquisitely
gowned in sea-green satin, her thick auburn hair,
freed from its tight bun, curled in riotous abandon
about her fine-boned face. Tiny diamonds sparkled

among the shining tresses and glittered about her throat.

"Well, what does he say, girl?"

Her aunt's excited voice shattered Catherine's daydream, and her common sense returned with a thud. It was the height of folly to even imagine for a second that one of the richest peers of the realm would deign to cast his eyes and hand in her direction.

"Why, Mama, calm yourself," Barbara dared to tease. She was safe for the moment from censure since she held in her hand proof of the earl's continued regard. "He says he has been wounded, but that it is naught to worry about." She waved her fingers dismissively. "He misses me, of course, and longs to be home again, though truth to tell I never could understand why he had to fight that beastly little Frenchman."

Wounded! Catherine paled at the news, a circumstance which, fortunately, went unnoticed.

Lady Carr's disappointment was clear. "Is that all? Did he not mention when he would be returning to London?"

"No. I do not believe so. I daresay soon." Barbara stared at her mother in puzzlement. "Is it of import?"

"You ask such a thing, Barbara? Surely you want to see him again!" It was her turn to be perplexed. Could it be Lord March was more of a threat than she knew? Maybe she misjudged the attachment between the two of them. Her blood ran cold at the thought.

"Has Lord March so turned your head you have forgotten your engagement? You will cease this foolish behaviour at once! You are betrothed to a peer of the realm and I will thank you, miss, to act the part if you cannot feel it naturally. Now take yourself out of my sight and reflect on your good fortune before I completely lose my temper."

Barbara flushed an ugly red, her lips thinned in anger, but even she did not possess the courage to disobey her mother's command. Jumping up from her seat, heedless of the pages of fine parchment in her lap which scattered to the floor, she flounced from the room. The door slammed with a bang which was heard from the cellar to the attic of the aging town house.

Superbly indifferent to the chaos she had caused, Lady Carr rose majestically to her full height and sailed out of the morning room. She was confident her wishes would be obeyed to the letter.

With the exit of her ladyship, the two younger girls broke into excited chatter about the scene they had just witnessed. With hardly a glance at their older cousin, they moved by mutual consent to the far corner of the room, where their giggles punctuated their awed murmurs and shocked exclamations.

Catherine was well aware of how little control she had over her charges. Unhappily her eyes dwelt on their young faces alive with the avid enjoyment of the past moments. How two such innocent-looking children, who both bid fair to being as beautiful as their older sister, could be so totally self-centred was beyond her comprehension.

When first she had come to the Carrs she had entertained high hopes of finding some measure of contentment. Her foolish dreams of being a wanted and useful member in her uncle's household were speedily dashed. True, the death of her mother's only brother had been a severe blow to his large family, especially in view of her own unexpected presence, yet still it was hard to credit the hostility she met at every turn and for no reason she was able to discover, try as she might.

It was not as if she were a beauty capable of arousing jealousy in the all-female household. Why, no self-respecting man would deign to give a skinny slip of a penniless girl with red hair and pallid skin so much as a passing glance. At least that was what Cousin Barbara had assured her knowledgeably when she had once timidly expressed a desire to mature and marry. Catherine was not to know how milky white her skin appeared in contrast to her auburn hair. Or how deep and mysterious her green eyes were as they changed with her moods—light as a summer sea when she was happy, dark as the deepest forest when she was worried or sad.

Catherine sighed wearily and rose from her uncomfortable chair. Since it was apparent the girls were content to entertain themselves for a while, she might as well set about picking up before her aunt caught her staring into space. She could still remember vividly the last scolding she had received for daring to daydream. Lord, how she longed for the freedom to read, to play the piano, or just to sit. Yet ahead stretched endless days of dreary tasks accompanied by shrill voices and sharp rebukes. She sighed again as she bent to gather the forgotten letter. Gravely, with meticulous care, she smoothed away each crease before securing the pages together. The feel of the expensive stationery and the sight of the bold strokes brought alive the image of the earl. Unable to resist the impulse to see for herself that all was well with him, Catherine glanced over her shoulder. Seeing the girls still engrossed in their speculations, she scanned the first lines of his letter. Forgotten were the rights and wrongs of reading another's post.

My Darling,
How I miss you. I haven't long before I leave, but I could not go into battle without talking to you. That seems strange to say when you are far away in London and I am here. Yet that is how I feel. I sit here and imagine you and I are married and home alone together, just the two of us. . . .

Catherine's eyes misted as she read of the love of the dark-eyed earl. If he had written such a letter to her, she would have treasured it beyond measure, yet

Barbara appeared unaffected by his ardent outpouring. Curiosity warred with caution as she gazed longingly at the remaining pages. She could not bring herself to read any more of this man's innermost feelings. Instead her eyes searched fearfully for details of his wounds while keeping a careful ear to the whispers in the corner. For some unknown reason, she had to know he was all right. She *must* know. Her questing glance locked on the shaky writing so unlike the rest at the end of the last page. The change in the sure even strokes told more than the words:

I was wounded slightly last week, my dear, so I beg your forgiveness for the lapse in my writing, as well as the delay in posting. Don't worry, it was nothing serious, I assure you. The duke's own physician tended me. Thanks to him, I should be well again in no time....

The sudden silence in the room warned Catherine that the girls were watching. Hastily refolding the stiff pages, she turned to find two pairs of sharp eyes staring at her.

"What have you got there, Cat?" Victoria questioned impudently as she walked slowly across the room to stop inches away. Her gaze was fixed on Catherine's hands.

*I am almost twenty and fully grown,* Catherine assured herself silently as she eyed the twelve-year-old. Knowing it was useless to correct Victoria's manner of address, nevertheless, she tried.

"Victoria, I do not care for your discourtesy. Have the goodness to apologize, please," she commanded as sternly as she was able. It was difficult to maintain her poise, recognizing her own guilt in the matter.

Ignoring Catherine's command, Victoria snatched the paper from her hands and dashed for safety behind the settee, holding her prize aloft.

"Barbara's post. Barbara's post. You were reading Barbara's post . . ." she chanted over and over.

Not to be left out of her sister's fun, Melissa added her lusty voice to the verse. It was asking too much of Fate to allow their concerted effort to go unnoticed by the household. In a matter of minutes the imposing presence of Lady Carr once again brought silence to the morning room.

"You will give that to me at once, miss." Lady Carr stood in the centre of the carpet, her eagle eyes fixed unblinkingly on the two miscreants behind the sofa.

Victoria shifted uneasily from foot to foot, her eyes darting about like a trapped animal. Catherine watched the scene, knowing that she was well and truly caught. Victoria was a sly thing who had got her into more trouble with her aunt than she could credit. Nine-year-old Melissa would follow her lead despite the fact that she was shivering with terror as she faced her mother. Catherine bowed her head, unable to bear the accusation Victoria would of course take great pleasure in making.

Victoria came slowly around the settee and advanced to her august parent's side. An artistically trembling hand extended the object desired.

Lady Carr eyed her daughter suspiciously. She was no fool and the change in her demeanour had not gone unnoticed, nor had she failed to observe her niece's distress. She recognized the pages in her hand at once. Something was more amiss than she had first thought.

"How did you come by this, Victoria?"

Catherine raised her head. She had done wrong. Now it was time to face the consequences. She could see at a glance that Victoria was well into her dramatics.

"It is the earl's letter," she began in a shaky whisper, barely audible in the silence.

"Speak up, child."

Victoria jumped a bit at the shrill command and, with a quick peep through her lashes, tried more boldly.

"Catherine was reading the earl's letter, Mama."

Lady Carr's mouth gaped in shock as her gaze flew to her niece. "Is this true, girl?" she demanded.

Catherine nodded. "Yes, ma'am." Her voice was a bare whisper, but remarkably steady for all that. She marked Lady Carr's alarming change in colour with awe. She looked fit for a seizure, or even murder. Her own, Catherine had no doubt.

The girls were forgotten. "Why, you miserable little chit. After all I have done for you, taking you into my home, treating you as my own. The nerve! The ingratitude! Count yourself fortunate I know my duty, or you would find yourself in the streets."

She sank onto a convenient chair to glare at Catherine. Belatedly she remembered her audience and her glare deepened. "Take yourselves to your rooms. I shall deal with you later."

Her promise of future punishment wiped the smirks from both faces as they practically fell over each other in their haste to escape.

Catherine stood straight, her thin body taut with her determination to remain unbowed. Every nerve tensed as the silence stretched ominously between them.

"So you seek to read your cousin's mail, my dear." Lady Carr's voice was quiet, gentle almost.

Here was very real danger. Catherine knew menace lurked in the hush. She had never known such fear. Surely a beating was kinder. She dug her nails into her palms to still the rising panic which threatened to reduce her to begging for mercy. She would not give Lady Carr the satisfaction of seeing her brought to her knees.

Her opponent was disappointed in her victim. The thought of Catherine's having the courage to pit her frail strength against hers fanned the flames of her wrath. The disdain and youthful dignity in those huge green eyes made her palms itch to slap Catherine's face.

"I think perhaps it is time to look about for another place for you to live." She paused to observe the effect of her words. She smiled in grim pleasure at the paling of the already white face. The chit looked ready to swoon.

Catherine's mind reeled at the dreadful pronouncement. She should have expected it, she realized vaguely. Blackness swirled about her, threatening her consciousness. Her aunt's next sentences sliced through the mist like so many knives.

"Marriage, 'tis the thing."

Catherine gasped aloud. "Marriage? But to whom? I know no one, let alone love any man, enough to give my hand in marriage." Startled out of her customary subservience by the enormity of her fate, Catherine forgot to guard her words.

"Love! Ha! More fool you! Who did you expect to love a penniless orphan living on the bounty of her relatives? It is not as if you have any beauty to recommend you," she exclaimed bluntly. "What I have in mind for you is a widower with a family to raise. 'Tis just the thing for you. Even taking into account your lack of dowry, it should not be too difficult to find you a mate in the ranks of the Cits. The name of Carr is most desirable to those who aspire to raise themselves above their common background. Rest assured, niece, married you shall be, and soon.''

Catherine made one final attempt to change her aunt's mind. Anything, even begging, was preferable to the fate which awaited her. ''Aunt, please reconsider. I will do anything, marry if you wish, but at least allow me the chance to find someone for whom I can truly care, as my parents cared for each other.''

Seeing her aunt's set expression, Catherine realized her plea was for naught. Her shoulders slumped in defeat.

''I see you understand,'' the older woman remarked. ''Besides, your marriage settlement will go a long way toward financing Barbara's wedding finery. It would simply not do for her to go to her bridegroom in rags.''

CATHERINE STOOD ALONE in the chill of her tiny attic room that night, her aunt's pronouncement still echoing in her mind. How she got through the remaining endless hours of the day, she did not know. Her whole body seemed devoid of feeling. She was certain that nothing could have the power to hurt her again. For the first time in months, she did not drop into bed exhausted to sleep fitfully beneath her inadequate blankets. She stared out her lone bare window at the black velvet sky and its glittering jewellike stars. Quiet settled over the old house like a gentle benediction, only the stately booming of the ancient clock on the landing disturbing the peace.

Her heart cried in anguish at the prospect of the future as she gazed sightlessly over the dark streets of London. Love, the one thing she longed for most, was as far out of her reach as the moon. Never to know the security and happiness of being desired above all others was not to be hers. The kind of warmth her parents had was to be denied her for the rest of her life. Tears streaked down her cheeks. The future yawned bleak and empty before her.

Mother to another woman's brood. Sold into marriage so Barbara might have a few more dresses to captivate her husband. The memory of the earl and his love for Barbara drew a cry of agony from the very depths of her being. She, who would value such a love as he offered beyond price, was denied the right.

Briefly she pondered the risks of running away. But even as the idea surfaced, she dismissed it. She had no money, few clothes and no friends from whom she might seek aid. Her age made her unsuitable for most positions, added to which she had no one to recommend her. She was well aware of the dangers which lurked in the streets for the unwary female, even for a drab such as she. At least marriage was respectable. She would not dishonour her parents' memory by shirking her duty to her aunt and guardian. As unpalatable as it was, her course was decided.

Striving to find some hope in the future, she brushed her tears away determinedly. In the dim light of the moon, her frailty and vulnerability were even more pronounced than usual.

A widower could not be too bad, or he never would have married in the first place, she reasoned silently. So perhaps all was not lost. At least there was one advantage—the absence of her formidable aunt and her brood—she thought wryly.

THE NEXT FEW WEEKS were some of the worst Catherine had known since coming to the Carr household. Everyone from the meanest scullery maid to the butler was aware of the plans afoot for her disposal thanks to the tattle-wagging tongues of the girls. It took all Catherine's strength to ignore the whispers and pitying looks from the servants. Even more unbearable was her cousins' frank delight in her fate. Barbara was over the moon at the prospect of a marriage settlement for her sole use, while her charges took every opportunity to tease Catherine over her prospective bridegroom's appearance, each description being more malicious and unpromising than the last.

Catherine observed the constant attendance of Mr.
Black, Lady Carr's man of business, and guessed the
search for an appropriate match was on. As the days
passed and her aunt's temper grew shorter, Catherine began to take heart. Perhaps even the Carr name
was not sufficient to overcome the obvious lack of
looks and dowry of the bride. Hope glimmered
faintly.

Lady Carr was so involved with Catherine's situation that Barbara's own peculiar behaviour escaped her notice. Catherine, however, was not so
blind.

For days she had unobtrusively studied her cousin.
The daily delivery of a single white rose was the first
sign. The fact that the flower came unaccompanied
by so much as a card clearly indicated the secretive-
ness of the practice. Though Barbara denied all
knowledge of the sender when questioned by her
mother, Catherine could not fail to read the pleasure in her eyes when she thought herself unob-
served. This, added to the frequent trips by her
cousin to the lending library for new books almost
every other day, aroused her curiosity. For Barbara
often proclaimed in her hearing that she would die
rather than read even a single novel.

Quite by chance, Catherine stumbled upon the
reason for Barbara's duplicity. Lord March! Seeing
his lean face bent attentively to her cousin's up-

turned eyes when they thought themselves unseen in the Park stirred her to anger as nothing had done before.

How dared they contrive to meet in secret, defying Lady Carr's wishes as well as convention! How dared Barbara betray her husband-to-be so basely with a man who flirted with any woman, be she wealthy, innocent or servant! Only the reality of her own position stayed her impulse to confront the cheating pair. What a fool she would look. Most likely she would be to blame for causing a scandal which would be responsible for Barbara's slip from grace. Nothing short of death would stop her aunt in her plans to recoup the family fortunes.

Catherine turned away to hurry home, helpless to save the man who invaded her thoughts with such alarming frequency. Her mind was so caught up in her inadequacy to aid the earl that she scarcely heard the lecture her aunt delivered on her tardiness with the floss she was sent to buy.

The fact that she had no earthly reason to wish the earl well or to recall his face so completely escaped her. All she knew was that she desired to see this man happy even if it meant marriage to her self-centered cousin. Though why, in truth, she had no idea. Perhaps the courage and uncomplaining acceptance of his duty to fight the French and risk death or disfigurement was the cause. Whatever the explanation it mattered not. She accepted her feelings as she did all other surprises in her young life. Given the chance, she would do her utmost to serve him.

# CHAPTER TWO

GULLS SCREECHED OVERHEAD, adding to the din of
the busy wharf. Marcus made his way to the moor-
ing of the ship which would carry him back to England. Although the predominant language was
Dutch, the small Netherlands harbour was true to the
nature of such places the world over. It was a noisy,
none-too-clean scene, with constant arrivals and de-
partures of goods and passengers. Surrounding the
motley collection of weather-beaten buildings, the
mid-morning air was redolent with the odour of de-
caying fish, rotting timber and unwashed bodies.
Every individual on the crowded dock was bent on a
destination or employed in some labour. Sailors
shouted warnings to pedestrians as cargoes were
moved to and fro.

Marcus stood out among the men around him, not
only because of his elegant dark grey coat topped by
a long black cloak, but because of his sheer presence. War had sharpened his air of command, re-
moving all traces of gentler courtly manners. His
lean figure drew many eyes as he strolled purpose-

fully up the narrow gangplank to the deck of the *Haarlem*.

He glanced about the small vessel, marvelling at the number of persons already on board. Near the bow was a Dutch merchant talking excitedly with a fellow who appeared to be an employee. Next to him, a young crippled man, obviously a returning soldier, stood staring morosely out to sea. A scattering of wives, young children and one or two businessmen completed the passenger list. To his right the open hold was a scene of much activity, as deck hands worked feverishly to lower the animal cargo, consisting mainly of the horses belonging to men such as himself, who were returning home, safely into the cramped quarters below decks. Marcus's keen eyes picked out his batman as the first of his two mounts was hoisted high in a rope cradle and swung down into the black pit. He was so engrossed in studying the tricky operation that he failed to note the covert glances and looks of pity his appearance created.

The weeks of convalescence at the camp, where every day he was witness to terrible scars and disfigurements, each more grotesque than the last, had inured him to the shocking effect of the angry red welt marring his left profile. The nagging anxiety over whether or not his arm would ever be fit for duty pushed what little concern he felt to the far recesses of his mind. Looks or lack of them mattered little when placed against the loss of an arm, a leg or both.

The first inkling he had of the attention he was drawing was the shocked exclamation of a young female voice. "Mama, look! What a terrible scar!"

The earl instinctively glanced around to see what drew the child's eyes. He took a step back, stunned, when he found himself confronted with a red-faced older woman clutching a girl's hand.

The woman curtseyed awkwardly, her embarrassment evident. "I'm sorry, sir. She is but a child and has not yet learned to guard her tongue."

Sheer surprise held Marcus speechless. Surely the injury to his arm was not noticeable. He flexed it self-consciously.

Nervous at the blank silence, the poor mother babbled on. "Anyone can see, sir, your face is still handsome," she offered in a blatant attempt to soften her offspring's words.

Realization dawned. My God! It was the scar on his cheek! Marcus quelled the urge to reach for the angry slash which still ached, especially when he was disturbed as he was now. The nagging throb aggravated his increasing discomfort. Good manners forced him to try to relieve the woman's unease, although there was little he could do to change the coolness of his tone.

"Do not distress yourself, ma'am. I quite understand. I have lived with my mark for so long, I did not remember."

The good lady's expression revealed her disbelief, but she seized the excuse gratefully. With a murmured thank-you, she quickly gathered her skirts and shepherded her daughter down the narrow steps leading to the lower cabins before her child could utter any more unfortunate remarks.

The earl watched the pair hurry away, his fingers straying to the puckered scar. For the first time it was borne home how cruel and unthinking people were to those returning from the battlefield. If a minor mark such as his was capable of eliciting such an unbridled reaction, then what was in store for the poor devils far worse off? Lord, how he wished he did not have to return without completing his goal. Only the lovely image of his Lady Barbara softened the blow of exile. She would never be so cruel as the two who had beat such a hasty retreat.

The ill-tempered snorting of his bay mare effectively dispelled the tenor of his thoughts. He turned back to see the sailors dodging her flaying hooves while trying to manoeuvre the nervous horse through the opening to the hold. Marcus breathed a sigh of relief moments later when the empty cradle emerged again. Now that he knew that his mounts were safe, he could retire to the doubtful comfort of his bunk and the solitude it offered. The days of travel from the battlegrounds in France to the sea coast of the Netherlands by horseback over rough and sometimes dangerous roads had taken their toll after his weeks of inactivity. His body, much to his disgust, ached more than he'd believed possible. He was bone weary, damned discouraged and certainly not looking forward to the overnight crossing to the coast of England, followed by more time in the saddle before he reached London.

As he carefully negotiated the steep steps to his cabin, he wondered vaguely if he was just being plain stubborn about his desire for speed by taking to horseback. His outspoken batman thought so, at any rate.

Opening the cabin door, Marcus ducked under the lintel and stepped inside. First-class accommodations, he thought with a wry smile, surveying his cabin. Thank heaven it was only one night. The bed was fit for a midget, not for a man of six feet. Every available space was utilized, from the compact dressing table on which his comb, brush and soap were placed ready for use, to the bunk with its movable rails for sleeping undisturbed during rough weather.

He tossed his cloak over the end of the bed and shrugged out of his coat with little difficulty, despite the stiffness of his shoulder. Once such a feat would not have been possible without Bates's diligent assistance. At least in this instance his weight loss was a decided advantage. With his batman-cum-valet keeping watch over the horses, he would have been hard put to do for himself in the matter of attire in his usually snug-fitting coats.

Marcus ran his hand through his hair as he sat down on the edge of the bunk. He grimaced at the boardlike pallet. "It is easy to see I won't get much sleep tonight, and I thought the camp bed was a rock," he lamented aloud.

Disregarding the clean linen, he leaned back and propped his feet up on the footboard. With a resigned grin he surveyed the length of his frame against the shortness of his mattress. It was all of a piece, he thought drowsily, his eyes closing slowly. Once he was back in London—ah, things would improve. Lady Barbara! Lovely, golden-haired Barbara. The warmth of her skin, the scent of her exotic perfume, seemed to fill his senses as he drifted into sleep.

A smile softened his features as he relaxed for the first time in days. He was oblivious to the shouts of the hands, as the aging ship slipped its moorings and eased out of the harbour.

Consciousness returned slowly as Marcus opened his eyes to the pitch darkness of the cabin. His limbs were stiff and cramped. He rose gingerly and flexed his arm, bringing a stabbing pain to his left side. How long would it be before the ache receded, he wondered in disgust.

A light tap on his door cut short his thoughts. He recognized Bates's knock and bid him enter.

"I heard you moving about, my lord," the wizened little man explained. He placed a lantern on the dresser and then proceeded to light the cabin lamps. "It's late—gone eleven it has—so I took the liberty of putting aside a little something for you to eat when you arose. Shall I bring it in?"

Marcus frowned. Nine hours he had slept. Had it been only weeks since he rode day after day with only a scant hour or two respite? Frustrated at the slow regaining of his strength, he paced the small confine irritably. Two turns, then he stopped, aware that Bates was watching him, still awaiting his instructions.

"I don't know what I would do without you, Bates," the earl sighed as he crossed to the tiny porthole to look out. "I am a bit hungry," he admitted over his shoulder. Repining on what could not be changed was a fool's choice.

"I'll be only a moment."

Marcus heard the click of the door. The star-studded sky outside held his gaze. After his experience in France, the frivolous, empty existence of the London social whirl no longer appealed. At this moment he could not think why it ever had. He wanted, no, he needed to do something worthwhile. He could not let his comrades nor himself down. The longer he stood looking out at the night the more firmly entrenched the idea became. But how? Crippled as he was, what could he do? He turned away from the porthole as Bates returned with a tray. Maybe Barbara would have some ideas. He smiled a little at the thought, feeling a bit less frustrated.

If he read the ship's progress aright, they should make Dover sometime after dawn. If he rode straight to London, he would see her the day after. He dug into his makeshift meal with an appetite.

Marcus's reckoning was accurate. The *Haarlem* docked early the next morning. Marcus strode off the gangplank confidently, at home with the sights and sounds familiar since boyhood. Even the loud voices and curses brought a smile to his lips. It was good to hear English again. Filled with an urgent need to be on the road, he had used his rank and wealth to receive preferential treatment. His horses were the first out of the hold.

The sight of Bates on the *Haarlem*'s deck wiped the smile from his face. The ringing echoes of the batman's outspoken objections to his wish to travel by horseback still sounded in his ears. He was fully aware of the debt he owed Bates for his unstinting care, but he was through being coddled. He had work to do, and what's more, Lady Barbara was waiting. He had no intention of returning to her less than the man she had accepted and given her hand. He was angry at Bates for implying he was still too invalid to attempt the trip alone. He damned him for an old woman.

Bates, however, had not entirely give up his protective ploys. "Might I not come, too, my lord?" he asked, scanning his master's face anxiously, his hand laid pleadingly against the neck of the earl's bay mare.

"Hell's teeth, man, be done. Am I not a man grown?" Marcus's patience was exhausted. He was as eager to be away as Delila, his mare. The horse sidled restlessly, her head jerking up and down in agitation.

The valet's expression reflected his hurt and his worry as he stepped back.

Seeing his distress, Marcus relented somewhat. "Take a damper. I'll come to no harm on a well-travelled road in broad daylight. Besides, you will only be a few hours behind should anything happen," he offered in consolation. With a wave of his hand he touched his mount lightly with his spurs, setting her into motion.

Bates nodded, unhappily aware there was nothing more he could do. He watched his lordship expertly guide the mettlesome Delila through the throng of pedestrians toward the open road, taking pride in his expert handling of the fresh mare. Perhaps his concern was for naught. The earl seldom misjudged his own strength.

Once free of the village traffic, Marcus urged the mare into a ground-eating canter. It felt good to be home in the lush green countryside of England. The miles flew by as Marcus alternately walked and cantered his horse. He kept cattle stabled along the highway, which enabled him to make frequent changes.

Toward afternoon the steady, rapid pace began to take its toll. He was still hours away from London, yet his shoulder ached as though he had been travelling for days. Each jar of his mount's step shot through him like a hot poker. By the time he reached the last hostelry before London itself, he was past the point of simply needing a respite. Sheer stubborn determination hauled him into the saddle one final time. Even the two glasses of brandy of which he had partaken while waiting for the horses to be changed did nothing to assuage the deep lines of pain etching his features.

The last bone-jarring miles passed in a haze. Instinct kept Marcus moving in the proper direction and years of riding kept him astride. Darkness was falling just as he reached the outskirts of the City.

"Not much farther now," he murmured, which was encouragement both for his horse and himself. Thank the stars he was almost there. He latched onto Barbara's enchanting face to divert his mind. Tomorrow. She was so close now. She would be so glad he was home again, for she had not wanted him to risk his life in France. How extraordinarily sensitive she was! How she had cried and begged him to stay when he had told her of his decision to fight for his country.

Marcus sighted the golden beacons of light surrounding the entrance to his town house. The sound of his horse's hooves on the cobbled streets scarcely had time to die away before he was ushered into his bedchamber and out of his travel-stained clothes. The familiar faces of his staff radiated welcome as they rushed to comfort and refresh him.

Drifting into an exhausted slumber, he realized how very fortunate he was. Although he had been

denied the opportunity to be there for the defeat of
Napoleon, he still had his loyal and trusted staff, his
friends and, above all, his golden-haired Lady Barbara.

It was well after noon by the time Marcus arose
from his bed. The long hours of rest had not left him
as recovered as he had hoped. Between Bates's dire
predictions regarding his ill-advised journey and the
sight of his drawn, haggard countenance in his shav-
ing mirror, he was in no mood to be sensible. The
stiffness of his shoulder further reminded him of his
crippled status. He would not let another day go by
without calling on his betrothed. With that in mind,
he donned his best grey superfine and light cream
breeches and ordered his curricle with its matched
greys to be brought round. Perhaps he would take
Barbara for a drive in the park.

CATHERINE DREW BACK, hidden by the shadows of
the house. Barbara, in the company of Lord March,
had just drawn up at the town-house entrance. If her
cousin saw her, she would be in for a severe scolding. So Catherine hid, unable to slip away until the
pair left.

"Here we are, my dear." Lord March turned to
Barbara, his voice pitched low.

"Will you come in?"

Catherine winced at the barely concealed eager-
ness in Barbara's expression. Lady Carr would not
be pleased.

"I think not, my lovely one. Your mother does not approve of me."

Barbara's eyes flashed with temper. She hated being crossed by anyone about anything she wished. "As if I care!" she exclaimed.

Catherine saw the satisfaction in Lord March's eyes. She almost had to pity Barbara for her self-centred preoccupation with her own desires. Couldn't she see that the man was playing with her? There was no love in his eyes, nor in his heart. He was nothing like the earl, a man whom a woman could trust with her honour!

"I mean so much to you?" he asked, leaning closer.

Barbara searched his face, seeing admiration there. He wanted her, she knew it. Her mother was wrong. "You know you do," she whispered.

"Then hold, pet. The time is not yet right, I fear." He stepped down from the phaeton without giving her an opportunity to reply.

"As you wish, Robert," Barbara agreed, sighing.

Catherine edged out of her hiding place. The pair being occupied with alighting from the carriage, she could slip around the corner and in the back door. Dodging quickly, she avoided all but the scullery maid and the cook's eyes as she entered. She arrived in the hall as Barbara came into the house.

Catherine was just in time to hear the butler greet her cousin. "Lady Carr requested your presence in the salon as soon as you returned, Lady Barbara."

"Very well, Jenkins." Barbara removed her sapphire pelisse and bonnet. Sighting Catherine hovering at the foot of the stairs, she signalled imperiously. "Come here, Cousin Cat."

Catherine tried to control her breathing as she crossed the space as slowly as possible. The rush to get back into the house had left her winded. Barbara might be self-centred, but she was sharp. The last thing Catherine wanted was her asking questions. She had little enough freedom as it was.

"Well, hurry up, girl." Barbara's foot tapped an angry tattoo, a well-recognized indication of rising temper.

"May I do something for you?" Catherine asked, her voice soft where Barbara's was hard and strident.

Barbara glared at her before thrusting the outer wear into Catherine's arms. "Here, take these to my chamber. And don't forget to hang them up properly. My maid says the creases never did come out of the last gown you put away," Barbara snapped spitefully. "Not that you would know enough about pretty things to realize the care they require."

Catherine swallowed her own temper. She had learned it was useless to fight the unjustified barbs tossed at her. Struggling against the tide of the Carr will was futile. No one listened and no one cared. She endured for she had no choice. But she would not sink to their level. Her parents had taught her dignity and endurance.

Barbara eyed her victim, liking the subdued look she wore, and in her arrogance missing the strength beneath. It pleased her to see the drab little chit so colourless, so without spirit. When Catherine had first arrived at the house, she had suffered a few sleepless nights wondering if she had a rival. Now she knew better, she thought complacently, surveying her golden blonde curls in the hall glass. Catherine, today, was a pale shadow next to the sunshine of her own beauty. Satisfied with the comparison, she tired of tormenting the mouse.

"Don't just stand there. Do as I say immediately."

Catherine breathed a silent sigh of relief as she hurried away. She had escaped detection. Two gifts today. One half hour in the garden to walk among the flowers and the small trees, and one less scolding. She smiled a little at the thought. She could almost hear her mother telling her that anything was endurable if one could look on the bright side. And tonight there was the book she had managed to secret from the library. And the small end of the tallow candle one of the maids had tossed aside. Two more gifts. Not a bad day at all. She paused on the landing for a moment, wishing just for a second she could have someone of her own, someone to talk to, to share with, someone who would care she had seen a mother bird with her babies today. She sighed, shaking her head at the foolish thought. She was here, and here was where she would stay until she

married to suit her aunt, unless a miracle happened.
The sound of voices got her attention. She leaned
over the railing to see Barbara just entering the salon without closing the door behind her.

"You wanted to see me, Mama?"

"I did." Lady Carr put down her sewing. "You're
late again."

Barbara shrugged lightly. "The Row was more
crowded than usual," she offered, carefully omit-
ting the mention of Robert's unscheduled stop in the
leafy tangle of one of the less frequented paths. Even
now the memory of his passionate kisses had the
power to bring an added sparkle to her eye.

"So you were with March. How much longer do
you think I shall countenance your behaviour? You
have chosen to defy me, meeting this man in secret,
setting up engagements with him without telling
me," Lady Carr hissed, reading her expression ac-
curately. "You're a fool, girl. A silly, green fool. I
thought I'd trained you better."

The acid words touched Barbara on the raw. It was
enough that Robert was taking forever to come to the
point. "I want to marry him," she shrilled in a rage,
forgetting herself.

Catherine's lips parted in shock. But what of the
earl, she demanded silently. He was a proud man. He
did not deserve such shabby treatment. Horrified,
she edged closer to the head of the stairs in time to
hear Barbara's impassioned declaration of love for
Lord March. The earl was such a gentleman. A

woman would feel safe with him. Lord March was a
rake, his dark eyes holding too much knowledge of
the world and the women in it. Catherine shivered,
remembering the day she had been alone with him in
the salon before Barbara had come down. He had
looked at her as though he could see through her
dress. She had wanted to hide that day, to pull a thick
blanket about her to shield her from his sight. He
had made no move to touch her, speaking once only
in a velvety voice she had found strangely mesmer-
izing. She had watched him as one would a wild animal. His smile had told her he recognized her fear
and liked it. That look had been the most frightening of all. She had never been so glad to see Barbara
than she had been when her cousin had arrived in a
swirl of velvet and rich scent, allowing her to escape.

The sounds of horses stopping on the street drew
Catherine's eyes to the door. Surely Lord March had
not returned.

It was the stroke of four as Marcus pulled to a
stop in front of the Carr family residence. He
scarcely noticed his groom's descent to the street as
he studied the dark burgundy phaeton weaving its
way through the crowded roads.

What could Lord March be about calling on the
Carrs? Surely his future mother-in-law knew better
than to receive a man with so noted a reputation for
flirtation. If he had learned one thing about his pro-

spective mama-in-law it was that she guarded her reputation and that of her daughters far more closely than an abbess.

The earl mounted the steps slowly as the butler opened the door. He handed his curly-brimmed beaver and gloves to the waiting footman. The austere butler's eyes widened as he took in the earl's altered appearance. Momentarily his usually impassive features registered his shock and pity before he controlled his expression.

Marcus noticed his reaction but paid little attention. Lady Barbara's loveliness filled his mind. "Is Lady Barbara at home, Jenkins?"

"In the salon, my lord, with Lady Carr. Shall I announce you?"

Marcus shook his head. "No, as long as they're alone, I believe I shall surprise them," he declared, heading for the open double doors to his right. As he reached them, he heard raised voices. Barbara. Lady Carr. Both were angry. He had never heard his beloved speak so harshly. Frowning, he paused on the threshold.

Catherine moved closer to the railing and peered cautiously down. The tall, slim figure below was surely not his lordship. Then a memory stirred as the visitor turned his head, catching the light. Indeed it was the earl, come home, safe. Unaccountably, her heart raced with joy. Until this moment she had not truly realized how important his welfare had become to her. A blush stained her cheeks at the direction of her thoughts. He was betrothed to her cousin. Unable to tear her eyes away, she watched him. The furious voices of her relatives made her wince. Such a homecoming.

"I won't have it, I tell you—" Lady Carr snapped her sentence off as she realized they were no longer alone. She gasped slightly as she recognized the earl. So astonished was she at his unexpected appearance she failed to notice his exhausted pallor or his injuries. Not so, Barbara. From her position, Marcus's scarred face was completely revealed. To her horrified eyes he was nothing at all like the man the ton called the English Adonis.

Marcus noted Lady Carr's uncharacteristic silence with a slight twinge of amusement, but Barbara was the one he had come to see. His eyes sought and found her, her back to the open window with the sun bathing her in what seemed to him an almost paradisiacal light.

He stepped quickly into the room, the smile on his face slightly crooked because of the wound. "Have I struck you dumb with amazement?" he asked quizzically, taking her hand in his and raising it to his lips.

Barbara was mesmerized by his actions. She could not take her gaze from his puckered cheek. Was this what he meant by a trifling wound?

The earl watched her face, unable to believe the horror and revulsion he found written on its beautiful surface. There was no mistaking her recoil as she sought to pull her hand from his grasp. Pain arrowed through him. The force was so intense he was beyond feeling for a moment as he released her. Love, it would seem, did not conquer all.

"You're back early!"

The hysterical edge to her words grated over his emotions. He flinched, recalling every expression of pity and disgust, every word spoken to him about his scars since he'd left France. Bitterness welled up at the unfairness, the cruelty, of the reactions. His Barbara, his love, his *life* did not want him.

"As you can see, my dear," he drawled harshly, "I could not wait to reach your side." He made no attempt to temper his sarcasm in his despair.

Lady Carr had been silent, thinking quickly. If her daughter was bent on making a byword of herself with Lord March, she intended to see she was safely married before she did. She had hoped that once Barbara saw the earl again, she would forget about her unsavoury suitor. She had not bargained for Barrington's altered appearance. Knowing the degree to which her offspring was repelled by disfigurement, she saw the earl's fortune slipping through her fingers. She had to stop Barbara from betraying herself further.

"Of course you couldn't, my lord," she rushed to say. "We are delighted, aren't we, dear?" She fixed her daughter with a commanding eye.

Barbara collected herself, agreeing hurriedly. "Yes, naturally we are."

Marcus stared hard at both women, seeing more than he wished. He had always known Lady Carr was more interested in the Barrington wealth and title than she was in him personally. The revelation that Barbara was equally shallow was a blow more crippling than his wound. At least her mother had the decency to be honest in her avarice. She had not recoiled from his scars.

"I must apologize for my unheralded arrival, but I had hoped I need not stand on ceremony with you, my lady," he explained politely, ignoring his fiancée completely.

Both Barbara and her mother noted the omission with varying degrees of dismay, and in Barbara's case, some relief. It was unlike Marcus to be impolite or rude to anyone. His manners were renowned by the ton for their correctness under any circumstances.

Lady Carr's smile was forced, her temper just barely held in check. Barbara wanted a good boxing. She shuddered at the thought of the future without the cushion of the Barrington wealth.

"Are you cold, ma'am?" The silky voice of the earl brought her eyes to his.

The earl no longer seemed the gentle, easy-going man she had known, Lady Carr decided. The war had changed more than his outward appearance. There was an aura of danger about him now. He stood erect, commanding the room and the occupants. Barbara had made a grave error. This man looked ready to follow his wishes regardless of those around him. Undecided as to what course to take, Lady Carr sat helplessly, watching her plans crumble before her eyes.

Marcus smiled slightly. "Perhaps custom could be stretched for a moment only, my lady. I wish a word alone with Lady Barbara." His future was altered beyond recognition. Had the choice lain with him he would have long gone from the room and the woman who had betrayed his love. But society and its rules must be served. A gentleman did not cry off regardless of the circumstances. He stared at his wife-to-be and added harshly, "I have much to say."

"That is unnecessary, surely, Mama," Barbara pleaded desperately, reaching for her mother's arm.

Lady Carr removed her daughter's hand. "Nonsense, my dear. There is naught improper in my lord's suggestion."

Barbara watched the door close behind her mother with dismay. Turning, she flushed a deep pink at Marcus's bitter look. "Shall...we sit down," she suggested, stammering in her nervousness.

Marcus nodded, steeling himself against the fear he saw in Barbara's eyes. For one fleeting moment he almost gave in to the need to touch her, to hold her and plead with her to accept him. His jaw tensed as he steeled himself to forget his heart and listen to his head. He knew her now as he had not in the past. There was naught left to him but pride and the small protection a beautiful wife—who had taken him to her bed despite his scars—could give him from the slings and arrows of society. He smiled grimly at the thought that he had been reduced to standing on his pride and vanity.

Barbara shivered at the smile on his lips. Without thought, she sat down on the pale blue sofa, which was a perfect foil for her blonde beauty. Fear and nerves kept her eyes modestly downcast as she sought vainly for a way to retrieve her position. There was no doubt she had blundered badly by allowing her distaste to show so plainly. Marcus was a proud man and would not forget the reaction.

The silence stretched between them. For his part, Marcus was in no hurry to speak. Was his pride worth the years of being tied to a woman who did not love him? Could he not use Barbara's horror at his disfigurement to his advantage so that she would cry off, thereby releasing both of them from an intolerable situation?

"It does not really appear that bad, Marcus," she offered, while being careful not to look at the wound directly.

Marcus glanced at her, one brow lifted sardonically. By her very words, she condemned herself. She would accept him, hating his touch, in exchange for the life he could give her. A need for revenge rose within him. She had caused him pain almost beyond bearing. Did she not deserve to share the fate she had meted out to him? "You need not pretend, my dear. We both now know what you want. My love—" he laughed harshly "—may have blinded me once. But no more."

Barbara's lashes flickered upward in surprise. Had he heard about Robert? "I don't understand."

"Don't you?" he returned softly. He observed her paleness with a kind of pleasure. Once he never would have considered causing her distress. "Never mind, you'll get what you desire, as will your mother," he decreed with some impatience. "Nothing has really changed between us. Your hand is pledged, my dear. Regrets or no, you've made your choice."

Barbara now found she could not take her gaze from his face. She was shocked by its coldness. There was no admiration, only a hard contempt which he made no effort to hide. Robert's face surfaced in her memory, his ardent expression a balm to her wounded pride. He loved her.

"I have decided to move the wedding up to the end of the month. Now that I am home there is no need to wait."

Stunned speechless at the crisp delivery of his intentions, Barbara shivered.

"You need not concern yourself about the bridal expenses. I am well aware of your family's dwindling resources. As for our marriage, well, since there is no longer any love on either side, we must live with what we have. I want an heir, a hostess for my table, and a helpmate. You need my money and will delight in the title, no doubt. A fair exchange, I believe." He watched her, outwardly cool while inside the pain burned with a fierce heat. For the first time he noticed the tiny flaws in her appearance he had overlooked in his infatuation. Had her eyes always been so hard, her mouth so thin, not the generous curve he had always imagined?

"You expect me to agree to these terms?" Barbara demanded incredulously. "To live with you knowing you hate me?"

"I now realize, my dear, you could live with the devil himself if it suited you. Witness how you reacted to my face." He stroked his disfigured cheek. "Yet you sit here expecting a few sweet words to change a situation of your own creation. Oh no, I am under no illusions." Forgetting his stiff left arm in a sudden burst of uncontrollable anger, he reached for her hand to drag her nearer. The awkward, jerky movement of his sore limb drew Barbara's eyes from his face in horrified fascination.

Barbara leapt out of his reach, her revulsion stronger than ever. "What's amiss with your arm? The merest scratch, nothing to be alarmed about. Liar! Liar! I won't live with a cripple. Even if you were the richest title in the land, I could not bear the fumbling of your hands or the sight of your face. You're mad to think that any woman would want you!"

Dark red surged under Marcus's exhausted pallor, driving out the grey tinge of his skin. He rose slowly to his feet, supremely conscious of the agony of his shoulder.

Barbara's gaze fastened on the scar as he moved toward her. A feeling of panic overrode her last remaining restraint. With a harsh sob, she evaded the hand he held out and snatched the Barrington family ring from her finger and flung it at his chest, where it landed with a tiny dull thud.

"Get out! Get out!" she screamed. Marcus stared at her through a black swirl of rage, pain and bitterness. What a fool he'd been! Without a word, he bent and retrieved the heavy ornate heirloom lying at his feet. The gold glimmered dully in his hand as he looked at it blankly. His mother's ring. He raised his eyes to Barbara's face, all expression wiped clean. The agony was too deep, too raw to show itself in the light of day.

"As you wish, my dear," he murmured, his voice flat. Scarcely favouring his left shoulder, he bowed slightly as though to a distant acquaintance, before he turned and walked out.

Catherine's eyes widened as Marcus entered the hall. She had heard every ghastly word. She ached to slap Barbara and to comfort the earl. She could do neither. She could only watch helplessly as a proud man faced his bleak future. Tears filled her eyes. She knew too well what it was like to lose everything one held dear. Like herself, Marcus was alone.

# CHAPTER THREE

CATHERINE SLIPPED QUIETLY into the empty schoolroom, thankful the younger Carrs were spending the day with their great-aunt. Her eyes glistened with unshed tears. Barbara's shrill words still rang in her ears. How could she? she wondered, stifling a sob. What kind of woman was her cousin? To cry off was terrible enough, but to do so in such a cruel fashion was unspeakable. As long as she lived, Catherine would never forget the look on the earl's face when he had left the drawing room. It was as though something vital in him had died. It had taken all her self-control not to leap out and try to comfort him. Huddling in the worn rocker in the corner, she tried to make sense of her feelings for a man she had seen only at a distance.

The sound of footsteps passing outside the door drew her attention. Lady Carr would not be pleased when she heard what Barbara had done. Her aunt had counted on the earl's money for too long. The whole household knew how empty the coffers were. The shriek of her aunt's voice carried all the way to the schoolroom.

"You did what, you silly chit?"

"I said I threw the ring at him. I couldn't bear the thought of handing it to him."

Catherine winced. The scene had been even worse than she had imagined. No wonder the earl had looked so devastated. In that moment she almost hated Barbara for her insensitivity. The earl's disfigurement was slight. His exploits and bravery on the battlefield surely had to be more important.

"You fool! You have ruined everything. The earl is beyond our touch now because of your stupidity."

"You forget Lord March."

"I forget nothing. The man means no good. It is not your hand he seeks."

"You're wrong."

"We shall see. Because of your actions we no longer have a choice. Bring him up to scratch if you can, but be quick about it."

Catherine huddled deeper in the chair. She knew how Lady Carr felt about his lordship. The whole house knew. For her to sanction Barbara's intentions was an indication that matters were indeed desperate. Lady Carr might be greedy and title hungry, but she loved her children, for all that she was prepared to see them married to men to enhance the Carr name.

"So this is what you do when my back is turned, miss," Lady Carr snapped, coming into the schoolroom unexpectedly. "Get down to the kitchen at once and lend a hand, you lazy, ungrateful wench."

Startled out of her thoughts, Catherine rose hurriedly. "Yes, Aunt." Knowing her aunt's temper needed an outlet, she was wary of moving closer for fear of having her ears boxed.

"Well, what are you waiting for?"

Catherine edged nearer, readying for a bolt past. "Nothing, Aunt," she answered, picking up her skirts and fleeing the room unscathed.

By the time Catherine reached the cook's domain, she was sadly out of breath. Sinking weakly onto the nearest stool, she missed the glances of concern from the two scullery maids. Catherine was a favourite with the working members of the house, with the exception of Lady Carr's and Barbara's maid. Her unfailing good manners and sweet nature were a marked contrast to the rest of the family. Below stairs she was treated as the lady she had been born.

Mrs. Dobbs, the cook, looked up from the pot she was stirring, her narrow face flushed from the mammoth stove's heat. She surveyed Catherine's pale features with a kindly eye. "Sent you down again, has she, lass?" she remarked in her thick Irish brogue.

Catherine nodded. "I'm to help with the meals until the girls return," she got out when finally she could speak again.

"Good, and I have just the task for you. How would you like to run along to the greengrocer's for me? I've run a bit shy on a few things to dress the duck."

"Really?" Catherine's eyes lit with pleasure at the thought of an outing. The animation brought a momentary flash of beauty to her pinched face.

Her benefactress smiled. "There's no need to rush, but mind how you go." She wiped her hands on her none-too-clean apron before drawing a crumpled list from its gaping pocket. "Here's what I need, and watch the count. Joe Thatcher's not above closing his eyes when he's doin' his tally."

Grasping the scrap of paper, Catherine took one of the maid's shawls from the hook by the rear door and made good her escape. Once outside the back gates, she paused to inhale deeply, enjoying the freedom of such a simple act. She strolled slowly down the street taking pleasure in observing the activity and scenery about her.

The small store was too soon in view. As Catherine stepped inside, she was glad to note they were extremely busy, with Nellie, her brother, Ned, and their ruddy-faced tyrant of a widowed father all engaged in serving customers. From long practice, Catherine faded into the crowded section of the store where Nellie was working. She had no desire to have either the owner or his burly son take care of her order. Either was certain to spoil her pleasure.

Catherine was unaware of the rosy flush on her cheeks from her walk or the unaccustomed sparkle of militancy in her emerald eyes from her suddenly rebellious thoughts. For the first time in a long, long while she would please herself. Yes, she would have Nellie serve her if she had to wait all afternoon.

It was well nigh that long before Catherine finally faced the youngest Thatcher across the counter. By now the shop was empty of all but a few stragglers.

"Mrs. Dobbs needs these, please," she explained, handing over the list.

Nellie grinned amicably. "Got a special dinner, has she?" she asked, glancing over the requirements.

Catherine laughed softly. "Not really. She is simply out of these things."

Catherine spent an enjoyable few minutes talking with Nellie as she filled the list. She was smiling as she gathered her purchases and turned to leave. She was almost to the door when she came face-to-face with the one man she did not wish to encounter.

Joe Thatcher stepped into her path, his small eyes running over her slender form. "Good day, miss."

Catherine shuddered slightly in the thin dress and shawl as he stared at her, her pleasure gone as quickly as it had come. Repulsed by the look in Thatcher's eyes, Catherine longed to run as fast as she could from this place.

"Good day," she murmured uneasily. "Excuse me, I must go." Without looking at the man again, she slipped past him and out the door.

She hurried down the street intent only on reaching the safety of her aunt's house. This time she glanced neither right nor left. The anticipation that had brightened her eyes was dead, killed by the leering eyes of Thatcher. Thank the good Lord she was not required to visit his shop often, she thought. He made her feel as though she had stepped in a mud puddle.

JOE THATCHER EYED the unadorned front of the Carr family residence with a certain amount of nervousness. All the night before and this morning he had planned what to say to the owner, his biggest debtor. It was easy enough to do in his own home, especially spurred on as he was by the news that the daughter of the house was no longer betrothed to Barrington. After all, he was a hard-working man and he had a right to his money, he decided with determination. He stepped boldly up to the front door and plied the knocker briskly. No skulking about for Joe Thatcher. It was his right to demand payment and he meant to have it one way or another. His ruddy complexion took on a darker hue when Jenkins opened the door. There was no mistaking the superiority of the older man's expression.

"I want to see Lady Carr," Thatcher demanded belligerently. "And don't try to tell me she ain't here 'cause I know for a fact she don't venture out this here door 'fore noon.''

Faced with a tradesman, Jenkins made an attempt to oust him from the front hall.

"The service entrance is around to the side," he suggested austerely as he held the door, waiting for the visitor to take the hint.

"Oh, no, you don't. I came for my money and I'll stay right here till I get it."

Short of throwing the man out, Jenkins had no alternative but to leave him where he stood. "I shall inform her ladyship you are here," he agreed reluctantly before mounting the stairs. He tapped on the outer door of the bedchamber and waited. When the dresser answered he explained his errand.

"Surely you can see to him."

"Unfortunately not."

The door shut in his face, leaving him standing in the hall. Moments passed, then it was wrenched open and he faced an irate Lady Carr.

"What is the meaning of all this commotion? Send the lout about his business. Why, I haven't even had my breakfast yet!"

"I'm sorry, my lady, but he won't leave," Jenkins murmured, holding his ground.

Lady Carr's bosom heaved alarmingly. Stalking out onto the landing, she glared down at the entrance and the bulky person seated there. Rage at the straits to which Barbara's ill-advised behaviour had reduced her filled her mind. Cursing her husband

and selfish daughter alike, she considered the situation. She had to keep her wits about her or they would really be in the suds.

"Show him to the back room. I shall see him there." She didn't wait to see if her orders were carried out before returning to her chamber.

Shown into the small room at the rear of the house, Joe was surprised he had got this far. Now if he could just get what was owed him. At least he was the first of her creditors, so the odds were in his favour. By late afternoon, the news of the broken engagement would be common knowledge, then there would be no getting near the door, let alone inside.

He scanned the luxury surrounding him, taking in the gold-framed hunting prints, the various bric-à-brac scattered about on the inlaid tables. It was hard to believe some of this stuff had not been sold to settle the pile of Carr debts. Quality were queer birds, he decided. He, who prided himself on owing no man, was looked down upon for being in the trade, while they lived like kings and owed their soul to half the city or more.

As he made his philosophical observation, Lady Carr stepped into the room. He rose, studying her carefully. "Your ladyship."

Lady Carr acknowledged his greeting with a nod, then motioned him to be seated.

"You wished to see me?" Her voice was cold, distant, not a tremor betraying her unease or worry.

"I did. I've come for my money. I've carried you as long as I can. It's time for the reckoning." He drew out a sheaf of unpaid bills. "Here's the tally of what's owed." He placed the stack on the desk in front of her.

Lady Carr barely glanced at the papers. "I am well aware of your due, I assure you, and it will be settled soon."

"Maybe it will, but then again maybe it won't. The way I hear it, you're penniless, and with your daughter's betrothal broken, you haven't a hope of making a recovery," he stated bluntly.

Her ladyship's face reddened with anger and humiliation. That she, a Carr, should suffer the indignity of this sordid business was beyond anything. "So, what do you suggest?"

He looked surprised. "We strike a bargain, what else? You give me something equal to the amount you owe and I give you these."

Lady Carr laughed harshly. "Don't you think I would have spared myself this if that were possible, you fool?" Rashly, she gave way to helpless rage. "I haven't got a thing worth even half of these." Her hand scattered the neat stack in front of her.

Joe's expression conveyed his contempt. "Think again, my lady. You have a fine house, though not in the best state of repair, and jewels, horses and servants. Do you expect me to believe you have nothing of value?"

"Everything like that went long ago. What you see are copies, fakes, past reproductions. With the exception of my stables, of course. Though I scarcely think they are of any use. Most of my horses are well past their prime," she confessed, drawing a perverted sense of satisfaction at his expression of shock.

Silence reigned as each contemplated the other. A soft rap at the door captured their attention.

"Come in."

Catherine stepped hesitantly inside, not realizing her aunt had a visitor. "Am I to bring the girls to the drawing room as usual, Aunt?" She kept her eyes downcast as she had been schooled. A prickle of unease teased her spine. Risking a peep beneath her lashes, she found her aunt staring at her strangely. The shift of Lady Carr's eyes to her right was the first hint Catherine had that they were not alone. She froze at the greedy stare of Joe Thatcher and just barely suppressed a shiver.

"Of course."

Catherine jumped at the abrupt words. Welcoming an excuse to flee, she backed out of the room, forgetting herself enough to slam the door behind her. She reached the back stairs before an instinct for danger warned her to listen at the door. She had heard the older women of the household talking. Joe Thatcher had an unsavoury reputation with the kitchen help, and the cook had warned her to stay clear of the man. She didn't completely understand the look in his eyes, but she did know her aunt was angry, but more than that, afraid. She had seen the exchange of looks between Thatcher and Lady Carr. She was somehow involved, of that she was sure.

"Nothing of value?" Catherine heard Joe Thatcher ask. "I think perhaps you should reconsider."

"Supposing I sanction the allegiance between you and my niece. What do I get?" Lady Carr questioned sharply.

Fear and pain for what her aunt planned for her future engulfed Catherine in a wave of misery. A sob blocked her throat.

"I shall clear your debts and settle a substantial amount on you when the ceremony takes place."

"Not enough."

Never had Catherine felt so defiled. Her aunt and Thatcher were haggling over her as if she were a mare for buying!

"I hardly think you are in a position to be too choosy."

"Let's be honest, shall we? I am in a situation where not only do I need money but also time. You, in turn, are able to provide me with the first and most probably the second. In return for which you stand to gain a noble wife, as well as a financial reward if my plans succeed."

"I thought you said you didn't have any money."

"I don't, but I soon shall if all goes well. If you'll listen until I finish you'll see what I mean."

"Go on."

"My daughter has lost the earl. That much you know, but what you don't know is that she has another suitor who is equally wealthy. What I propose is this. You settle my debts and do your utmost to silence the rumours. That will give Barbara enough time to bring about her plans. Once she is safely married, Catherine will be provided with a dowry and you two may have my blessings."

"I'll agree, but with one small stipulation. I don't wait for your daughter's marriage. I want..."

Catherine grew colder as the discussion of her future continued. Her aunt must hate her to wish her wed to such a man as Thatcher. Footsteps sounded on the stairs. She edged deeper into the shadows, praying no one would see her. A moment later one of the maids passed and she could breathe again. Knowing she dared not linger any longer, she peered cautiously out. Seeing the hall empty, she scurried quickly up the stairs to the relative safety of the schoolroom.

The rest of the day passed in a fog of numbing coldness. Nothing seemed to penetrate her consciousness, not the malicious teasing of her charges, nor the temper tantrums of her older cousin. She longed for the privacy of her room. She had to plan what was to be done.

Every time she saw her aunt, she expected to be told of her fate. As the days wore on and nothing was said, she was torn between hope and despair, praying each night that her aunt had changed her mind. Toward the end of the week, the household was at sixes and sevens. Two days earlier, Lady Carr had announced the throwing of a large party, and Lord March was to be one of the guests. There was an unmistakable air of anticipation and Barbara was in such a good mood that all in the house were at pains to step lightly about her, not wishing to destroy the temporary peace.

Catherine was perched on a stool in the kitchen helping in the preparations. Freed from the onerous duties of shepherding the younger Carrs, she enjoyed the friendly, uncomplicated warmth of the big kitchen.

"I don't believe we have ever had such a grand party," she observed with a smile.

"Cor, no, 'tis a wonder we've this one," replied the youngest of the scullery maids with an impudent grin. "'Course an' we wouldn't have if'n ole Thatcher hadn't tore up Lady Carr's debts and come across with some blunt."

"That's enough, girl," the cook admonished. "Get on with your washing. Pay her no mind, Miss Catherine."

Her happiness dimming, Catherine shuddered at the mention of Joe Thatcher. His beady eyes haunted her dreams. She had half convinced herself that if her aunt had really meant her for the man, she surely would have told her by now. Knowing that Thatcher had in effect paid for the party was proof she could not ignore. Danger. She could feel it, taste the fear on her tongue. She had to protect herself. She had to find a way out of the situation. Anything was better than what she would suffer at the hands of Thatcher. Her only hope lay in Barbara's attaching Lord March. Surely even he would not countenance a connection with a common shopkeeper.

Catherine wished she dared slip from her stool and seek refuge in the schoolroom. But there was still work to be done in the kitchen. The chatter of the other girls barely impinged on her unhappy thoughts until one of the upstairs maids mentioned the earl.

"So what did you hear? Tell me," the youngest of the scullery maids demanded avidly.

"They say he shuns the sunlight like some evil night creature. He never goes to parties nor visits his friends. Wears black everywhere." The voice imparting the knowledge was full of relish. "My lady—" the sneer at the title was unmistakable "—told her maid it is but foolish gossip. But what could she know, her with all her airs and fine clothes?"

"I heard tell he gambles, recklessly, but he never loses. Drinks, too, yet he is never drunk. Ain't human. Folks say he carries the mark of Satan."

The cook turned from the pot she was stirring to fix the members of her domain with a stern look. "Mark of Satan—what nonsense! The earl got that scar in France—in battle. As for his luck, Lord March never loses, either, and no one puts him in company with the Devil. Now stop chattering and finish your work before Lady Carr tosses the lot of us on the street.'' She glanced at Catherine. ''And you best be on your way to the schoolroom, miss, before the girls arrive.''

Catherine slid from her perch, her mind whirling at the disclosures. As though it were yesterday instead of three weeks ago, she remembered the look on the earl's face when she last saw him. She had longed to tell him that any woman privileged enough to be loved by him, would not care a button for his battle scars. In fact, to her, they were badges of courage and honour, not ugly horrors to be hidden away in the darkness. The intensity of her need to reach out to him was almost a living part of her, and as natural as breathing. It didn't matter that he did not know her and never would. He was the embodiment of what she wanted in a husband: gentle, sensitive, kind and brave. In that moment her course was set for the future. If Barbara could not attach Lord March tonight, then she, Catherine, would seek her place elsewhere. She could not allow her aunt to give her into marriage to Joe Thatcher.

Feeling vaguely comforted, she entered the schoolroom and prepared to deal with her unruly charges, made even more so by the activity downstairs.

''When may we go down?'' Victoria demanded for the tenth time in as many minutes.

''After all the guests have arrived,'' Catherine answered. Reading the rebellion in her eyes, she continued, "If we go too soon your mama will see us or worse still one of the guests, then we would be banned from the landing completely."

Victoria stared hard at her for a second as though judging the truth of her explanation. With a sullen shrug she flopped in her chair. "So what shall we do until then?"

"Read or play with your dolls." Catherine bent down to retrieve a discarded sash, feeling a momentary return of her earlier dizziness. Not now, not again. She straightened, carefully praying she wouldn't swoon. Her aunt would not forgive her if anything spoiled this ball.

Melissa stood watch at the door and gave a running description of the arriving members of the ton. Catherine listened carefully for the first mention of Lord March. There was none. Frowning, wondering at the omission, not daring to ask Melissa or to show any interest in the proceedings below, she waited. For once Victoria was a help.

"What is his lordship wearing, Missy?" Victoria asked, shouldering her sister aside. "I can't see him. Where is he?"

Melissa shook her head. "I don't know. I didn't see him come in."

"Don't tease. You know Barbara invited him."

"I'm not teasing. He isn't here, I tell you."

"He must be." Victoria glared at Missy.

"Stop it, at once, ladies," Catherine commanded. "Your mother will hear."

"She's lying. Make her tell," Victoria demanded, turning on Catherine.

Missy was almost in tears. "I'm not lying. Barbara came out on Uncle Vincent's arm. You know she would not have done that if her lover was here."

Shocked at the plain speaking, Catherine stared. "Melissa!"

"It's true, Cousin. You're just not pretty enough to know anything about them, that's all."

"That's enough, Victoria. One more word and *you* will remain here while *we* watch the dancing." Catherine ignored the taunt, too worried over her own plans and the absence of Lord March to care what Victoria said.

"It's safe to go out on the landing now," Victoria announced. "Everyone is in line waiting for the guests to appear."

Catherine moved to the door to check for herself. Victoria wasn't above lying. "So they are. All right, be silent and stay near." She knew their nods of agreement had little to do with her influence. It was their healthy respect for the weight of their mother's hand that held sway.

Catherine stared down at the scene in the entrance to the small ballroom. Barbara stood beside her mother at the head of the receiving line. She was more beautiful than usual in the shimmering ice-blue gown with its daringly low-cut bodice. The Carr sapphires echoed the colour of the dress and set off her golden hair. But the jewels were as false as Barbara's smile. Catherine looked closer, reading the suppressed rage in her cousin's expression. It was not difficult to tell that Barbara had not known that Lord March would not attend. Suddenly Barbara froze, staring at the foyer.

Catherine turned and almost gasped aloud when she saw Lord March. On his arm was the most stunning woman Catherine had ever seen. She watched in dread as the crowd parted before the magnificent pair, allowing them to make their way unimpeded to Lady Carr's side. It was impossible to ignore the gathering's blatant interest.

Catherine regarded her aunt with reluctant admiration as she addressed the man her daughter hoped to marry, without betraying the slightest sign she noticed the avid gaze of the multitude. Even her attitude to the uninvited dark-haired beauty at his side could not be faulted. And miracle of miracles, Barbara followed her mother's lead.

Little though she liked her cousin, Catherine felt a twinge of pity. Lord March had chosen the most unkind way of all to make his intentions known, not only to Barbara but to the ton, as well. His performance was little short of public humiliation, and it would have been a total defeat for Barbara had she given way to her blazing temper.

As for herself, the die was cast. She had no choice. It would be tonight.

# CHAPTER FOUR

MARCUS STEPPED DOWN from his coach in front of one of the wildest gaming halls in town. Until a few weeks ago, he had hardly been aware such places existed in London. Gambling had been an amusing diversion in his salad days, but even that had been confined to the better-known and more exclusive clubs of the fashionable set. Now he found the roll of the dice and the turn of the cards his sole source of activity if not enjoyment.

Best of all, none cared what he looked like as long as his pockets were deep. There were many such as he who sought forgetfulness in the dens of vice which abounded in the back streets of the city. Here everything had its price, but at least a man knew what he bought.

The dark green door was opened by a burly porter who, in all probability, doubled as a bouncer when a client became too foxed to be manageable. Marcus shrugged out of his midnight cloak, revealing a black coat and breeches relieved only by the white of his shirt. The candlelight in the hall was kinder by far to his scarred face than daylight, yet it could not soften the gaunt hollows in his cheeks nor the newly formed lines of cynicism.

Having been to the same establishment the night before, he moved confidently up the staircase to the suite of rooms on the second floor. He entered the first chamber, an apartment given over to deep basset. He stood for a moment framed in the doorway, idly scanning the room. About a dozen or so people were seated around a single table, so intent on the game that his entrance passed unnoticed. Silence prevailed, broken only by the whisper of cards against green baize and the murmurings of bets. Seeing no empty chairs, Marcus moved on to the adjoining salon.

Here the noise was a sharp contrast to the room he had just left, the action more robust. Most of the furnishings were shabby green velvet, and there were a number of tables and stands for the punters' rouleaux and their glasses. There was a faro bank in full swing at one end and an E.O. table at the other. It was to this latter that Marcus made his way, pausing only long enough to take a glass of champagne from a passing waiter.

On the next turn of the wheel, he placed a hefty wager. Lounging in his chair, his eyes on the spinning wheel of chance, he paid scant heed to those around him. When the ball finally stopped, he was the winner. At least Lady Luck, unlike Lady Barbara, looked favourably on his suit, he thought cynically as he left the stack where it lay. At the questioning look of the woman presiding, he returned a curt nod to spin again.

As the ball bounced its way around the wheel, Marcus sipped his wine indifferently. Again and again he won. Soon the crowd around him grew as the gamblers in the adjoining salons caught the scent of his amazing luck. Amid the increasing excitement, he appeared curiously untouched, only the glitter of his fathomless eyes betraying any sign of life.

It was nearly dawn when he strolled out of the hall, his pockets weighted with thousands of pounds won in rounds from E.O. to basset. The sight of his carriage brought the first real hint that a flesh-and-blood man existed beneath the composed exterior. The champagne and brandy he had consumed with such abandon had finally come home to roost with a vengeance. The idea of jolting and clattering over the cobbled streets definitely did not appeal.

"I shall walk," he called to the coachman.

The man nodded silently before guiding the coach down the street, matching his master's slow progress.

Marcus, his senses swimming from the sudden contact with the cool morning air, headed toward the more fashionable section of the city. His senses cleared slightly. He was going to have a devil of a head shortly, and probably feel extremely unwell into the bargain. Not that it mattered much, since all he intended doing when he got home was sleeping until supper. By then it would be dark and safe to go out again. One distinct advantage to his reclusive way of life was that he had no appointments to keep—no one to answer to, he thought with bitter humour. The shadows were now his friends.

At the moment, however, the brandy still had possession of his brain. He felt detached from the things around him, his path home determined by instinct alone. The dawn was the maiden day's blush for the sins of the night. Drawing his cloak tightly about him, he sauntered up the alley behind Brook Street. It was an indication of his bosky state that he failed to recognize the back of Barbara's house until he stumbled slightly and had to pause to right himself.

A muted creak above his head drew his attention. A mass of white cloth flopped over the narrow sill to dangle to a stop a few feet over his head. He should walk on, he told himself, but didn't. His remoteness allowed only mild curiosity to intrude.

He watched in dazed fascination as a slim figure, apparently a schoolboy, wriggled his way backward out of the window and began a stealthy descent. Apparently just becoming aware of the skimpy nature of his escape route, the lad floundered at the end of the makeshift rope. Trying to find a toehold, he swung wildly, losing his grip on the sheet. With a gasp of fright, he landed, a tangle of flailing arms and legs, in the earl's arms, which had instinctively reached out. The unexpected assault caused Marcus to stagger. It took a full second for them to regain their breaths.

Catherine stared up at her rescuer, recognizing him instantly, despite the changes in his appearance. Blessing every saint she knew that he had never before seen her, and so did not know who she was, she prayed he would help her escape and not turn her in.

"What are you about, boy?" Marcus demanded, peering at Catherine owlishly. "Thieving?"

Startled at the mistake in her gender, Catherine stammered as she answered. "Oh . . . no." His error spawned a mad idea, a desperate chance of putting some distance between her and this place. "I am in service here. From the country," she improvised wildly. "I wish to return, but my mistress will not allow it, as she says it costs more than I am worth."

Marcus studied his catch gravely. He wasn't so foxed that he didn't know the situation was highly irregular, to say the least. The story sounded a lie, but taking into account the multipatched breeches, the coarse dirty white shirt covered by a threadbare dark jacket that were little more than rags, he was inclined to believe the youth. Besides, he thought as he looked up to glare at the house of his former love, it would serve the Carrs right to deal with the irritation of a missing servant. And the youth could be just telling the truth, knowing of Lady Carr's financial straits.

He glanced back to the pinched features beneath the peaked cap and decided the rescuing of the lad would suit him for the moment. The huge eyes darkened by the purple shadows beneath stared back at him, touching a cord in him, a soft spot he thought dead. He didn't like the feeling. Frowning, he caught the boy's shoulder and propelled him toward his coach. He had an idea he would regret his need for the petty revenge.

"Come on. If we stand about here, you will be found."

Had Catherine the strength, she would have jumped for joy. He would help her. She climbed into the coach, then hugged herself to stave off the chill of the early morning. She knew the earl did not live far from their house, but maybe, for this day, it would be enough.

Marcus stared out the window, wondering at his quixotic impulse. Fool! He turned his head, glaring at the child across from him. The weary slump of the youth's shoulders and the shadows under his eyes disturbed him. Lady Carr was a dragon and as mercenary a matchmaking mama as may be, but as far as he was aware she did not mistreat her staff.

The coach pulled up in front of his St. James' Square residence. He hardly glanced at the imposing facade as he alighted, without waiting to see if his companion followed. He passed through the hall to the study, where a fire still burned, Catherine close at his heels.

"Sit down," he directed, placing a taper on the desk and taking the chair farthest from the light.

Catherine did as she was bid. The journey and the escape which had proceeded it had sapped her meagre strength. She couldn't remember a time when she had felt so tired.

"Who are you?" Marcus demanded from the shadows.

Her lashes flickered open. She stared at him, trying to judge his mood. Nothing in his voice gave a clue. Should she confess her identity or carry on with the charade? She opened her lips to lie and then realized she couldn't, not to him.

"Catherine. Catherine Carr."

For a full minute there wasn't a sound in the stillness. Catherine began to doubt that he had heard her. Then he moved and she knew fear for the first time in his presence. He seemed to lunge out of the darkness to loom over her like an avenging angel. She drew back, knocking the cap from her head, sending her hair tumbling down in an auburn cloud.

Marcus stared at the curling mass, his hands catching in the cascade as he reached for her shoulders and pulled her upright. "Don't lie to me, girl. I want to know just who you are and what you were doing. If my face frightens you, close your eyes, but speak."

Catherine gazed into his eyes, transfixed at the harsh tone and the less-than-gentle way he held her. In all her dreams he had been tender and kind. Had she been a fool to believe in him? Had she been so lonely and in need of someone, even a dream someone to hold on to, that she had created one who did not exist?

"I *am* Catherine Carr. Lady Carr is my aunt. Barbara is my cousin."

"You're lying."

"Knowing how you must feel about the Carrs, why would I?" she asked simply. "I'm running away, though I'm not certain to where, for I have no one to go to." A look of pleading suddenly crossed Catherine's face. "Perhaps, sir, you will help me?"

"You can't stay here," he declared in response to her outrageous demand. "It's impossible. And why should I help you, anyway?" He raked his right hand through his hair, frustrated and yet not able to stop the whispering of his conscience every time he looked at her.

Catherine had nothing left to lose. "I won't go back. I don't care where I go, but I shall not return." She had meant to be firm, but the fear and desperation that had driven her from her aunt's house laced terror through her words. "If you try to make me, I shall kill myself."

"Quiet, you silly fool. Do you want to wake the whole house?" Marcus snapped, shocked at the wild threat. He looked at her closely, seeing things he had missed. She was almost beside herself with fear. He had seen too many men in battle with such wild eyes not to know that she was near the edge of breaking. Drawing a calming breath, he stifled his temper. No matter who she was, he would have no part in pushing her further.

"Suppose you start from the beginning and tell me why you ran away. Then we can decide what is best to be done."

Catherine gazed at him, suspecting a trick. He had no reason to offer her shelter, none to help her or to care what became of her. Yet he seemed to offer all three, at least for now.

"How old are you?"

The simple question acted as a spur to her tongue. "Nineteen. I shall be twenty in the spring."

Startled, Marcus sank into his chair. He had thought her a mere girl, not a woman grown. His head was ringing, and he cursed the impulse that had made him walk home and the even greater folly of putting Catherine into his carriage.

"You are not a child."

"I know. That is why I ran away."

He blinked. He knew he shouldn't have drunk so much brandy. Champagne he could handle, but brandy wreaked havoc with his mental faculties. "You will have to explain, slowly. I am not myself, I fear."

Catherine settled deeper into the chair, the warmth of the fire and his voice gradually unravelling some of the tension from her body. "Are you ill? Do your wounds still hurt?"

"I am foxed," he stated baldly, in no mood to mince matters. "I'll have a devil of a head in a few hours, not to mention the headache of you in my house.'' He shrugged, knowing he shouldn't have spoken so plainly, but not regretting the words. If the chit took offence perhaps she would leave and save him the trouble of deciding what to do with her.

"Father taught me a remedy," she murmured hesitantly.

"Spare me." Marcus groaned, feeling worse by the moment. "Just get on with your tale while I can still concentrate."

Catherine wanted to protest but thought better of doing so. He looked truly ill. She would not add to his discomfort more than she had.

"My parents were killed in a carriage accident soon after my sixteenth birthday. Since my father was a teacher, we had little money, so that when I was left alone there was no one else to take me in but my father's brother.

"My aunt made it clear from the start that I was to share in the household duties, but I really didn't mind. As a child I often dreamed of having sisters of my own and I thought my cousins..." She paused for a minute, her mind crowded with thoughts of her life in her aunt's house. She remembered that first night she was taken to the bare little room on the top floor away from everyone, even the servants, as though she were someone to hide. How lonely, bewildered and lost she had felt.

Marcus recognized her need to talk and did not interrupt. Every memory was mirrored clearly on her face. His interest was caught and held. She was such a tiny thing, all eyes and wild hair, and so incredibly frail. He scarcely heard her words as he pondered the twist of fate that had thrown them together.

"...and then last week I overheard my aunt bartering my hand in marriage to Joe Thatcher. She needs the money, you see, for Barbara. I would have done it if I could have liked the man even a little. But he is loud and cruel and he looks at me..." She shuddered, unable to complete the picture. Suddenly, the nearness of her escape and the danger in which she still stood was too much. The tears started. Huddling in the chair, she covered her face with her hands and wept, sobs tearing through her slender frame with the force of a storm.

Stunned, Marcus was slow to react. Her cries were causing him a pain he had not expected. If she continued to weep with such abandon, he feared she would make herself ill. Glancing around the room, he spied the brandy decanter and pushed himself out of his chair. Just the thing for them both. Splashing a small amount in one glass and a more bracing restorative in the other, he hurried to her side. Kneeling in front of her chair, he called her name. When she didn't answer, he gulped down his drink—after all, he needed a free hand—then dropped the glass on the floor. Pulling her hands down, he murmured soothing words which made no sense but seemed to calm her.

"I want you to drink this." He held her wet fingers tightly and waited for a hint she had heard him.

Catherine couldn't look at him. She was appalled at her loss of control. She had never liked watering-pot females. "What is it?"

Marcus's lips twisted in a faint smile. "Believe me, you would be best not knowing. Just trust me." He lifted the glass to her lips. "It will burn a bit going down, but it will steady you."

Catherine sipped the pungent liquid, coughing a little as it left a fiery trail in her throat. By the time she had consumed the glass, she felt a tingling warmth spread through her, making her light-headed. Thoughts and worries fled. For the first time since the awful nightmare had begun she was at peace. There was no need to think or to fight the sleep wrapping around her like a warm, cosy blanket.

Marcus sat back on his heels, watching the colour seep into her face, pleased he had given her some relief. Frowning at the thought, he considered the situation. Catherine was too innocent to know the consequences of her being in his home unchaperoned, but he was not. If one word of her stay leaked out she would be fit for nothing but the muslin company. His frown deepened. He shouldn't care, but he did. Such a tiny thing and so alone. She had to have help. But a Carr! Anger rose, and he remembered humiliation. Unknowingly, he allowed his hands to tighten on hers. Then he withdrew them abruptly.

Catherine's eyes fluttered open. His expression held no kindness, only a dark anger and pain. Driven to help him, she struggled to rise. She could see he was remembering. Her presence had brought the past alive. Swaying a little as she got to her feet, she forced the words from her lips.

"I'll go now."

Marcus's blank gaze followed her unsteady progress to the door. Her hand was on the knob before he actually realized what she was doing. It brought him to his senses. Nothing had really changed. The child still had nowhere to go, no one to protect her. To turn her away was tantamount to murder. And, heaven knew, he had not been reduced to that yet.

"Wait!"

Catherine froze, her eyes glistening with tears.

"You can stay here, with me...." Marcus spoke absently, his mind suddenly clear. There was only one way. Marriage. He needed a wife. What better way to have one and not bother facing the social whirl to find one? Revenge. He considered that, too. To elevate the poor little cousin to the title to which Barbara had aspired was a fitting punishment for what he had suffered at the Carrs' hands.

"You said you were prepared to go through with a marriage if you could at least like the man. Did you mean it?"

Catherine turned, unable to believe she had heard aright. "I did." She moved back toward the light.

"Would it matter that you did not know the man?"

"I don't understand." Catherine was only a step away, staring at him, feeling hope build but afraid to give in to the feeling.

"I am offering you my name and my protection."

Too shocked at the notion to guard her expression, Catherine's lips parted in astonishment. "You can't be serious!"

He nodded grimly. "Oh, but I am. Despite this—" he fingered the scar on his cheek "—I am still a man and I wish to start my family, have a wife to grace my table and stand at my side."

"But you don't know me. I have nothing to bring to you."

"Excuses." He glared at her, thinking that even though she desperately needed what he offered she was not prepared to tie herself to a cripple. He gave her credit for having the kindness to cloak her refusal in less-stark terms than her cousin.

"No." Catherine suddenly realized what he was thinking and hated the fact that he believed her capable of such cruelty. "It is not this." She reached up to touch his scar.

Her jerked back from her hand. "Leave it. I guess your need was not as great as I thought—"

"I'll marry you," Catherine interrupted before he could retract his offer. Clasping her hands tightly together, she awaited his reaction.

Marcus had control of his expression, and neither by look or word did he betray his relief. "So be it. For what little there is left of the night and for the morning you will stay here. This evening after dark we shall leave for the country. The ceremony will take place there."

Catherine was beyond being affected by his changing moods. Her future had a silver lining. She would be safe with a dream she had never expected to come true. She had no illusions. Marcus had other reasons for helping her than just for herself. She could see the anger in his eyes and the need to lash out at fate. But she would make this misfit match work. If it were within her power he would never regret taking her to wife.

Marcus indicated the stairs leading to the private quarters. "You will use my room for now. My man can be trusted to keep his lip still, but I can not vouch for the rest of the house."

They entered the master bedroom together. She stopped just inside to survey the splendid proportions and the opulent furnishings. The room was dominated by a great bed on a raised dais, curtained in lush, dark blue velvet. Long windows along one wall were similarly treated, while the furniture was a graceful combination of bygone eras.

"You will sleep there." His hand indicated the bed.

"I can not. That is your bed. Where will you sleep?"

"You need not worry. I shall not force myself on you either before or after our marriage. For now, think of me as a brother if you can," he suggested bitterly. "I shall sleep in the dressing room over there."

Catherine's gaze followed the flick of his hand, seeing for the first time the connecting door on the opposite side of the room. She wanted to tell him how he had misunderstood her, but he did not give her the chance.

"I'll find you something to wear, then I'll leave you. Don't worry about anyone disturbing you. The room I'll be using has its own door." He turned away and disappeared into the dressing chamber.

Once out of Catherine's sight, he stopped and leaned against the glass, his face contorted with a confusion of emotions. He was a fool, but his words could not be called back. He was betrothed to little more than an untutored child. He would have his wife, but what manner of wife, and at what cost to both of them? He straightened, knowing the course was set now. He, like the chit in the other room, had no real choice. He could not continue as he was, and she, for better or worse, needed him. Reaching for a shirt, he braced himself for all the tomorrows which lay before him as he reentered his bedchamber.

"This should do." He handed her the garment without looking at her. "Sleep well." Leaving without a backward glance, he shut the door firmly behind him.

Catherine stood for a time without moving, the soft silk of his shirt pressed against her breasts. It was odd how the worst moment in her life had led her to this. She had no idea what the future would hold. Marcus might very well regret his proposal later in the morning. But for now, there was someone who wanted her, although she didn't fully understand why. For now she would sleep in a soft bed, free from nightmares and cold. For now she was safe.

# CHAPTER FIVE

MARCUS SLUMPED IN THE CHAIR beside the narrow bed. Hell's teeth, he was tired. The click of the outer door brought his head up, a wary frown marring his brow. He relaxed upon recognizing Bates.

"Is it very late?" he asked, glancing at the the window. He had long since dispensed with Bates's services on his nocturnal wanderings, much to the valet's oft-voiced disapproval.

Bates halted in the doorway, his face conveying his surprise at finding the earl in the small room. "It is, my lord," he affirmed, coming over to remove the earl's boots. "I would have come to you. There was no need for you to wait for me here." He helped him out of his close-fitting evening coat, being careful not to jar his arm.

Marcus concentrated on the task, cursing the lingering weakness even as he strove to hide it. Catching Catherine had done his injury no real harm, other than to cause it to burn like the fires of hell itself. He sighed when he was free of the garment, glancing at Bates speculatively. The valet was devoted to him, having proved his mettle in all manner of circumstances, not the least of which was his refusal to stay behind in London when Marcus had volunteered for service. He could and had trusted Bates with his life. Discretion was the man's middle name. But stern disapproval was his first, and Marcus knew that Bates would object most vehemently when he heard about the presence of Catherine in his bed. Bates had a fine distinction about the right and wrong of ways to go on.

"I shall sleep here today," he announced, wondering if loyalty was worth the aggravation it oft times cause. "We have a lady visitor and I have given her my bed. It is imperative that the rest of the house remain in ignorance of her presence. I shall trust you to see to it."

Bates stared at him, his mouth agape and, for once, mercifully was silent. "You cannot be serious, my lord," he finally sputtered.

Marcus smiled grimly. "Oh, but I am." Attired in his nightshirt, he sat down on the edge of the bed. He shook his head in a vain attempt to clear it. "I suspect that last brandy was a tactical error. I have not had my wits about me, I fear." He pointed to a chair. "Sit, man. You are giving me a crick in my neck to match the ache in my head."

Bates sat, hard. "Beg pardon my lord, but I do not understand."

"Of course you do not," Marcus agreed testily. "I have not explained. The lady in there—" he flicked a hand in the direction of the master suite "—is soon to be my wife."

"Wife?" Bates was past amazement. He was nigh into shock. "Who is she?" he demanded, forgetting himself completely.

Marcus noticed the slip but refrained from pointing it out. "The girl is Catherine Carr." He acknowledged the valet's start with a grimace. "Barbara's cousin, penniless cousin, I should add. To put it bluntly, she has run away. Lady Carr is trying to force her to marry a person named Thatcher, a tradesman of some sort, and by her description, a totally unsuitable candidate for a well-bred girl of nineteen. She has been badly treated in the bargain, not physically, perhaps, but there are worse ways."

"Why did she come to you?"

"She did not. Or to be more precise, not by design." For a moment there was faint glimmer of a smile on his lips. "She dropped into my arms from a knotted sheet tossed out a window. Do not look so shocked. You could not expect her to walk out the front door with portmanteau in hand."

"No, of course not," Bates agreed faintly.

"The thing of it is that the chit has no clothes."

Bates's mind boggled at this bit of news.

"I want you to get her something suitable for the journey to my country estate."

"I? I know nothing of such things."

"Certainly you do. You dressed me in my youth as I recall." Marcus laid back on the couch, completely unaware of the visions dancing in his valet's head. "After you arrange for a dinner tray to be sent up promptly at five this evening—make it exceptionally well laid, for the chit is bone thin—I want you to find a pair of breeches, a shirt, a hat to cover her hair and cloak. It's bound to be cold on the road. I shall take care of the rest. Have I forgotten anything?"

"I'll need to know the size," Bates said, slightly red about the ears. Men's garments on a female. Had his master taken leave of his senses?

"About Tim's build, I would hazard," he murmured, naming the youngest of his second cousins.

Bates nodded, then got up to leave. "Shall I pack a portmanteau for you, as well?"

Believing he had handled the most pressing of his problems, Marcus was drifting off to sleep. Bates's question brought his eyes open. "Of course. I cannot get married without the proper attire," he muttered sleepily before turning on his side. "Don't forget to lock the door on your way out."

Bates stood indecisively in the doorway, his eyes straying to the door to the master suite. He could not sit idly by while the earl was hurt by another of the Carrs if it was in his power to scotch the scheme. Edging toward the entrance, he kept a wary eye on the earl. Never in all his years of service had he resorted to spying on his family, as he called them privately. But he would now, not that the Carrs were family yet . . .

Bates eased open the door and stared at the earl's bed. A crack of dim light between the window draperies illuminated Catherine's delicate features. She was nothing like the other one, he observed with some relief. In fact there was no resemblance at all that he could see. Thin as a rake, too, and no beauty to recommend her. Her looks fitted her story, anyway. Just pray she was different in personality, as well. One witch in his lordship's life was quite enough.

IT WAS AFTERNOON by the time Marcus surfaced from the depths of slumber. He opened his eyes cautiously in deference to his throbbing head. What the devil was he doing on the dressing-room couch? he wondered irritably. Surely Bates had taken leave of his senses by allowing to go to sleep here. He must have drunk more than he thought. Niggled by a fleeting memory, he tried to recall what else had occurred. Something important, of that much he was certain. Thoroughly annoyed at his inability to capture the elusive event, he jerked back the sheets.

"Good afternoon, my lord." Bates came softly to the earl's bed, bearing a tray with coffee.

Marcus eyed him dourly. "What is the hour?"

"A bit after one. The lady has not stirred yet this morning, though," Bates supplied helpfully as he handed the earl his cup.

Marcus sipped the dark liquid gratefully. "What lady?" he asked, giving scant attention to Bates's words. Egad, but the coffee tasted good, one of the few pleasant things to come out of his experiences on the continent.

"Miss Catherine, my lord. Surely you have not forgotten," Bates responded sharply, taken aback by the question. "I have the clothes you requested, as well."

"Catherine? Clothes?" Marcus stared at the valet, jumbled images passing through his mind. A pinched face with great cat-green eyes. A boy who was no boy at all. "My god, it is true! I thought it was a dream, a nightmare." He closed his eyes with a groan. He would never drink brandy again. "Are you certain she is still here?"

Bates reddened. "I have not looked in on her this afternoon," he replied evasively.

Marcus lurched to his feet. Maybe the chit had left. Damnation, but he hoped so. He unlocked the connecting door and swung it open. The room was dim, but there was light enough for him to make out the slight form under the sheets. Compelled by a kind of morbid curiosity to look upon the face of his future bride with a sober head, he advanced slowly toward the bed.

The girl's gentle breathing scarcely disturbed the stillness as he stopped a few inches from her side. He gazed at this creature to whom he'd offered marriage. She was as pale as the sheets on which she lay, her only colouring the tangled wealth of reddish hair. Her lashes were long and dark but they did little to detract from the gaunt hollows of her cheeks or the dark bruises under her eyes. He was more than foxed last night if he considered taking this...this female to wife. He could not forget his reasons had had more to do with settling the score with the Carrs than with the girl herself. But that was not sufficient enough an explanation for what he had done. The only excuse he had was that he must have been completely cast away. Fit for Bedlam.

There just had to be another answer for the girl and himself. He struggled to recall what she did at the Carr house. Children! That was it! She taught the nursery set. Just the ticket, he decided in sudden inspiration. He heaved a gusty sigh of relief. For a moment there...

He would take her to the country as planned, but he would not marry her. She wouldn't be happy anyway, he rationalized, too far out of her depth. Probably frighten her, send her into a decline or some such. Big house to run, servants to handle. No, the best thing was to find her a nice snug position somewhere, a couple of small children to care for with a country family. His bailiff was bound to know someone, and if not, he could enlist one of his cousins to help him secure her a post.

He nodded, pleased with his solution. He would give her some money to be going on with, and come to think of it, she was going to need a gown or two.

Being careful not to make any noise, he returned to his dressing room. In his concern for Catherine he momentarily forgot his own plans for evening the tally with the Carrs.

"I'm going out for a while, Bates. Stay right here until I return. I don't want Catherine awakening and giving her presence away."

With Bates's assistance he was swiftly attired and ready to set out on his errand.

The dressmaker's would be his first stop. He wondered briefly where a governess went for her gowns. Mayhap she made them herself, not that it mattered, he supposed, as he was the one handing over the ready in this case. As Marcus guided his curricle through the crowded streets, he concentrated on plans to extradite himself from the tangle of his own making and still settle Catherine satisfactorily. For once he was oblivious to the stares of those around him. Though he no longer participated in the social whirl of his set, he did drive out on occasion. He did, however, try to avoid the busiest time of the day, as it was now.

"Walk them," he ordered, tossing the reins to his groom as he leapt lightly to the street in front of Madame Celeste's, one of the most exclusive and popular couturières in London. It was a measure of his distraction that he had not sought a less-fashionable establishment.

Once inside, he was shown discreetly into a back room by an assistant, who, while perhaps aghast at his scarred face, had the wit not to mention it. When Madame heard who awaited her, her eyes lit with the thought of the money she was about to make. Although the earl had not been of late, he was an old and valued client, not only because of his late mother's frequent visits, but of his own discreet purchases for his amours. He never failed to order the best and what's more paid for it promptly, an almost unheard of practice among his set.

She smoothed her coiled hair, fluffed out the skirts of her dress and went out to greet him. "My Lord Barrington, this is an honour," she breathed in her best French accent.

Marcus had his back to the door as the little woman entered. When he turned, she gave an audible gasp and completely forgot her supposed ancestry.

"Cor, me lad, them Frenchies ne'er did that!" she exclaimed. "I 'ope you killed the bloody pig. If ye didn't, I shall."

The earl's face tightened at the first gasp, but her bloodthirsty reaction was so totally unexpected he forgot his disfigurement and laughed heartily. The sight of Celeste's round face and thistle-light body bringing down even one French soldier was the fable of David and Goliath all over again. Feeling better than he had in weeks, Marcus regained control and explained enough of his problem to make his needs clear.

Celeste nodded. "As it 'appens, I 'ave just the thing," she said, her French accent once again in place as she clapped for one of her menials. "Go bring me that dark blue serge *cherie*, and be quick. I would not 'ave such a thing in my shop, but it was to be included in an order for one of my customers for her niece who enjoys gardening." Her tone clearly indicated her distaste for ladies of quality who dug in the dirt like common peasants. "The girl did not like the colour." She shrugged is a purely Gallic way and turned to accept the dull, night-blue garment she had requested. She held it up for Marcus's inspection.

He studied the drab gown critically. Certainly not a becoming creation, he decided, but it would do for his purpose. At least, the size appeared near right.

"It will do. Also the appropriate underthings, your plainest bonnet and a dark cloak," he added. He could order the rest of what Catherine needed when they arrived at Barrington Court. Right now the important business was to get Catherine out of the city without discovery. He had not missed the curiosity in Celeste's eyes. His careful explanation had sounded lame even to his own ears.

*"Certainement,"* she agreed. "It will be only a moment while your things are wrapped." She signalled for her assistant to see to the rest of his requirements. "Shall I send the bill round?"

"No, that won't be necessary. I shall pay it now."

"As you wish, *monsieur.*"

Marcus silently cursed the need for discretion. The variance from his normal method of payment was certain to raise the woman's suspicions.

"Marcus, I did not think to see you here!"

Marcus started at the sound of Barbara's voice, and he turned slowly to face her. He caught his breath. She was even lovelier than he remembered. Her golden hair was topped by an extravagant confection of blue feathers and tulle that framed her exquisite features to perfection. The revulsion he had seen in her eyes at their last meeting was gone. The sapphire depths held all their old promise, and something more. An appeal, perhaps? He wanted to believe that was so, he realized in shock. Then, angered at the knowledge that his heart still responded to her, he forced himself to remember her last words to him. He had been a fool once. Not again.

"Lady Barbara," he greeted her coolly, making no attempt to face her fully as courtesy demanded. Unconsciously he kept his scarred left side hidden.

The only sign Barbara gave that she noticed his barely polite greeting was a slight narrowing of her eyes. Barbara moved closer, her voice lowering slightly. "I've missed you, my lord."

"Indeed?" Marcus inhaled her scent, finding it bittersweet. It seemed to cling to him, touching him in ways he did not wish.

Barbara frowned at the single answer. "We are at sixes and sevens today. I just had to get away."

Marcus's senses went on alert. For a moment he had forgotten Catherine and her escape. "A problem?"

Well pleased with his interest, Barbara smiled and leaned toward him. "It is my cousin. My mother gave her a home and now she has run away, the ungrateful wretch. Mother is nearly beside herself with worry."

"And you?" The earl watched her, fascinated in a way he had never been. She was completely without conscience or tender feelings. The hard glitter in her eyes was no longer masked by her extraordinary beauty.

Silently cursing the curious eyes of Madame Celeste, he watched her take one more step nearer. "I came away. There was nothing I could do, and all that confusion was giving me a frightful headache," she murmured in her sweetest tone. She glanced at Marcus, using her lashes to the fullest extent modesty allowed. "I have ordered a gown for a party next week. My favourite blue again."

Marcus flinched at the softness of her voice, drawn against his will to listen. He did not like her, knew her for what she was, and yet he found he could not yet escape her hold. How she taunted him, in his dreams and now this. Had he not likened her to a goddess in blue? The sweet scent she wore surrounded him in a silken web. Then he recalled Lord March and the rumours he had heard of her plans to trap him into marriage. March had not come up to scratch as yet, playing a wily game of his own. His heart hardened as he cursed himself for a fool. Taken in by a pretty pair of lips and a fragrance mixed by mortal hands. Barbara would use him if he let her. Her pride would prefer marriage even to one such as he to the ostracism of society, or another failure and mounting debts. Turning from her, he spoke to Celeste.

"I must depart. Another engagement."

He had to get out of the shop before he forgot his treatment at the shallow beauty's hands and succumbed to her soft promises of heaven cloaking the reality of hell. Was he a weak-kneed fool who begged for rejection yet a second time? He could not tarry. Catherine's haunted face, surprisingly vivid, surfaced in his mind's eye. She, too, had suffered from Barbara's cruelty.

"Ah, my assistant comes now," Celeste murmured in relief.

Barbara laid a hand on Marcus's arm while glancing at him through her lashes. "Marcus, will you not talk with me? Has my foolish tongue and the shock of seeing you hurt given you such a disgust of me that you cannot find it in your heart to forgive me?" She turned slightly so that her back screened them from the openly listening modiste. "I know I do not deserve a second chance, but I plead for one nonetheless."

"That's impossible, Lady Barbara. I have lingered longer than I intended," he answered curtly, facing her for the first time. The light from the shop's front window illuminated his scar in devastating detail. "I have urgent business which requires my complete attention for the next few days." This time the revulsion Barbara was unable to conceal caused little pain. His suspicions more than confirmed, Marcus collected his parcel and strode from the shop.

The earl's curricle rolled to a stop as he stepped onto the sidewalk. He tossed the package to his groom and leapt to the seat. His man scarcely had time to settle himself before the equipage was pulled away at a brisk trot.

# CHAPTER SIX

MARCUS TOOLED HIS HORSES expertly between the slower-moving vehicles, intent on putting the disturbing encounter behind him. Though his mind now recognized the shallow, spoiled creature behind the lovely face, his heart refused to forget his dreams. His blood ran cold at the thought of meeting her again and again. He almost wished he were married. Then, and only then would he feel some measure of peace. Not that there was a woman alive whom he felt the slightest urge to take to wife, he thought grimly, remembering the first week after his broken engagement when he had made an attempt to reenter the social whirl. No one had been quite as cruel as Barbara, but he had not missed the way eyes turned from him, the way whispers followed in his wake, conversations paused then continued nervously when he neared. Worse still was the pity, the shallow attempts at sympathy and understanding. By the end of the week he had ceased to go about, too disgusted to make any attempt at the most unexceptional outing. Now he preferred the night and the creatures who lived in the shadows. The women there were not so nice in their sensibilities. Thinking of the waifs and orphans of London brought Catherine's face to mind.

Catherine. His mouth twisted in a rueful grimace as he turned up Brook Street. His fiancée of the moment, though he had been foxed when he proposed. She slept in his bed, even still. The bed he had intended for Barbara on their wedding night. Suddenly he grinned. In the comfort of the gathering dark, without the fog of brandy to cloud his thoughts, Marcus contemplated his future. God knew the chit needed him. Barbara would be beside herself with rage, her pride in the dust when she saw the penniless cousin she despised raised to the wealth and title which she had allowed to slip through her fingers. As for himself, what better way to ensure his safety from Barbara's devious schemes and his own folly?

Moments later, he stood at Catherine's bedside. She was lying in the same position as before. He studied her in repose. This afternoon and in the very early hours he had scarcely seen her as a person. He retained only a vague image of her piquant face. It was only fitting he should study her now. After all, she would soon be his wife. Momentarily, he wondered, as he watched her sleep, whether he was a fool to tie himself to her for life. He knew he was no coward. France had proved that. Maybe he wronged himself and the poor girl he sheltered.

A low moan interrupted his thoughts. "Oh, Mama, please, please don't be dead...so lonely... tired...so very tired," the soft voice trailed away into a low, indistinct murmur.

Marcus stood still, caught by the pathos of her situation. Suddenly it was important he protect her. She was alone, defenceless without his aid. He could not help but admire her courage in running away as she had. No, for better or worse, a bride she would be. Having made his final decision, the earl put aside all his misgivings. There was much to be done and evening drew near. He stepped closer to the bed and lifted one work-roughened hand.

"Catherine. Wake up." At the sound of his voice, she stirred restlessly, then was still.

Marcus tried yet again, more loudly. "Catherine, you must get up. It is time we were away."

This time he felt life move in the limp hand he held. Slowly her eyes opened to look blankly on him. He waited patiently as she struggled to full consciousness. Finally, recognition dawned.

"It was not a dream. I truly did it?" she whispered. She took her eyes from his face for a moment to survey her surroundings. The opulence of the room was a far cry from the stark walls and tiny window of her own.

"If you refer to running away, then, yes, you did indeed succeed," he answered quietly, watching her carefully.

Catherine's gaze flew back to his face, his scar of little consequence when he spoke so gently and looked at her so intently. Her heart fluttered in her breast, reminding her of feelings to which she had no right and which he would not welcome. Fragments of his proposal echoed in her memory. Had he truly offered her his name and protection? Or had he come to tell her he had changed his mind? In the light of day had saner counsel prevailed?

Marcus read the doubt in her eyes and responded to it. "No, I have not regretted my offer," he said firmly, ignoring her look of surprise. "That is why I woke you. Bates brought up some hot water and there are clothes for you." He gestured toward the bundle on the foot of the huge bed. "You should find everything you need. When you're ready, tap on my door. Then we shall dine and be off. The roads will be dark then, less crowded."

Catherine was fully awake. "Clothes. But I have clothes," she argued in confusion.

Marcus's lips curled faintly, leaving her no doubt of his opinion of her ragged attire. "For a beggar-boy, perhaps. No, Bates has secured you a better choice. Once we are free of town, you will be changing again. I have bought you a dress." For a fleeting moment he regretted the dull gown he had purchased, then dismissed the thought. He would deal with her wardrobe later. "You will arrive at Barrington Court like the lady you are, and my future wife."

Catherine stared at him, sorting through the plans. Only one thing held sway. "You bought me a gown? You should not."

Marcus frowned, seeing her embarrassment. "Who else?" he demanded, irritated by her show of scruples. "We cannot worry about propriety now." Egad, was there ever such a tangle! "You cannot buy for yourself had you the money, which you don't. If you can sleep in my bed wearing my shirt then..." He let the hard facts of her predicament sink in.

Catherine whitened at the brutal assessment. He was right, she acknowledged fairly. What good were the rules now? If she had followed them, she never would have run at all.

"I beg pardon. You are right, of course," she whispered chastised.

Marcus nodded. "I shall leave you. Do not linger. We have quite a distance to go."

Catherine watched him move quickly to the door without a backward glance. Slowly a tear formed and trickled down her cheek. She had angered him with missishness. What a fool she was! Had he not pledged himself to help her? While she, like a brainless idiot, complained of his manner in accomplishing her escape. She got up from the bed and moved to do his bidding. She had no patience with foolishness. She had made her choice, aligning herself at his side. He had, for reasons of his own, chosen her for his bride-to-be. Together they must make a marriage. Another of her mother's adages was, Begin as you mean to go on. Well, she would begin. Tonight. Wiping the tears from her eyes with the back of her hand, she slipped out of his shirt and sponged down before donning the clothes Bates had brought. When she was done, she tapped lightly at the connecting door and waited for his command to enter.

"Shall I do?" she asked hesitantly as she turned slowly.

Marcus looked her over carefully. Her reputation and his depended upon getting her out of the house undetected. "Yes." Secretly, he thought she made a better-looking boy than girl. Undernourished and slight as she was, she had few female curves. Realizing the direction of his thoughts, he berated himself. This marriage was an expedient escape for them both. He would do well to remember that.

Catherine watched him anxiously, unsure what to do. She saw the approval he expressed over her attire die and that hard look she was coming to dread return to his eyes. Her heart sank. What had she done to anger him?

"Is something amiss?" she whispered, wishing she understood him better. She would give anything to please him, rather than be a burden when he was doing so much for her.

Marcus looked up, suddenly conscious he had been frowning at her. He noted the worry in the green eyes fixed so intently on his face, the trembling lips and tightly clasped hands.

"Stop that," he ordered sternly, his eyes black with anger. "No one is going to beat you or yell at you." He was unaware of how formidable he appeared.

Catherine was powerless to stem the tears which trickled slowly from her eyes. She had not meant to cry. She wanted to turn away but could not. His eyes held her prisoner.

Appalled at what he had caused, Marcus crossed the space between them in two long strides. He gathered her in his arms and pulled her unresisting body close to his. She was so small, little larger than a child. He was all kinds of a fool to frighten her. It wasn't her fault, after all.

"It is all right," he murmured soothingly. "If I am ill-tempered, it is not because of you, believe me."

He held her gently away so that he could see her face. He brushed her damp lashes with gentle fingers. "Do not cry anymore. I have faced the enemy in battle with more courage than the sight of a lady weeping," he teased, wanting to see the first smile on her face. Without realizing it his own lips curved slightly.

Catherine searched his expression, seeing a glimpse of the man he had once been, before the war and Barbara had done their work. "I have not always spent my life as a watering pot," she whispered back, an apology and a hesitant attempt to respond to his mood mixed in one.

"Have you not, my lady?" he queried, glancing down at his wet shirt. "Then it must be my poor self that sets you all on end."

"Oh, no, my lord!" Catherine heard only the words not the tone. "It is I, for I am still a bit tired and, it would seem, easily overset." Pulling from the warm haven of his arms, she made herself move away.

Marcus was puzzled by her withdrawal. What had he done? Surely the chit was not worried he would take advantage of her. If she intended to maintain this new guise, then so be it. At least she had ceased weeping.

"I believe that Bates will have our dinner brought to us by the fire. Shall we go in?"

He gestured toward a door on the opposite side of the room which Catherine had not previously noticed. She preceded him into the sitting room. Awed at the magnificence and luxury, Catherine paused to stare. The fireplace along one wall was a massive affair, complete with a gleaming marble mantel supported by twin columns. A fire blazed within. Amber velvet draperies were drawn across the long windows, creating a cozy atmosphere.

Marcus glanced at Catherine when he realized she was making no move to take a seat. The amazement on her face gave him pause, until he recalled her youth and the shabbiness of the Carr house. Sympathy stirred, and a vague doubt as to the wisdom of the course he had set. He would ask much of her, more perhaps than she could give. Then he shook the thought aside. What choice did either of them have? Turning away from her open, vulnerable face he went to the table and looked over the repast which Bates had brought up.

"I did my best, sir," Bates apologized, clearly not certain of his selections. "I know little of these things."

"You have done well. I have stretched your talents this past day," he added. "First you must needs keep me company in battle and now my latest start. Were I you, I would seek employment elsewhere."

Bates grinned, liking well the compliment and its delivery. "Well, as to that, what would you do, my lord?"

"Let us hope I need not find out." Marcus glanced over his shoulder. Catherine had not moved a step. "Come. Let us eat. The food grows cold."

Catherine started at the sound of his voice, then hurried to the chair which Bates held. She smiled nervously and thanked him before gazing at the laden table. She had never seen so much food. There were two entire birds roasted deliciously brown, a plate of paper-thin slices of ham, bread still warm from the oven, fresh berries, thick cream and a lovely plate of biscuits and cheeses. A veritable feast to her untutored eye.

"Is all of this for us?" she asked in amazement.

Master and servant exchanged glances over her head. In that moment Bates made his allegiance known. The budding protective instinct of the earl was not lost on him. And Catherine, young and unschooled as she was, had shown him the courtesy of the earl's late mother. In short, she had touched his heart not only for her potential as a great lady which he sensed, but for the influence she already had over his lordship.

Marcus took his place across from Catherine. Reaching for his wineglass, he waited while Catherine was served first. The deep-red Burgundy slipped down his throat easily, bringing a measure of relaxation. What a time the past twenty-four hours had been! And there was still more to come. The valet finished with Catherine's plate then reached for his.

"Leave it," said the earl. "I shall serve myself and Catherine for the rest of the meal."

Catherine eyed Marcus doubtfully. Why was he sending Bates away? Had she blundered again, gawking like a schoolgirl? Suddenly the delectable array before her lost its appeal.

Unaware of Catherine's uncertainty, Marcus helped himself sparingly to a bit of ham and a small portion of chicken. He looked up from his plate to catch Catherine's gaze fixed on him. "Is there something amiss?"

"No, no, of course not," she denied quickly. She was a fool, she berated herself. If she cringed and jumped every time he spoke, she would anger him for certain. He had promised he would take care of her.

It was past time she believed him, trusted him to keep his word.

Puzzled, Marcus asked, "Then why aren't you eating? Surely you are hungry." Catherine was such a strange mixture. He did not understand her, which was unsurprising as they were, in truth, strangers. Odd that it mattered to him what she thought.

Unable to explain, Catherine picked up her fork and forced herself to begin. She was hungry and it did smell delicious. For a while neither made any attempt at conversation. Catherine was too tongue-tied to know what to say, while Marcus was too preoccupied with his plans for his marriage to pay more than cursory attention to his betrothed's needs. It was only when he had finished and leaned back to light a cheroot that he consciously recalled her presence. He studied her for a moment through a thin haze of smoke, realizing he had not even asked her permission to indulge.

"You must forgive me," he murmured, leaning forward to crush out the cheroot. "I should not have done this with you in the room. A bad habit, I fear, picked up on the continent."

Catherine stayed him with a hand on his arm. Her gesture was impulsive, but her words were not. "Please. In truth, I quite like the smell," she said. "Besides, this is your home. You are sharing it with me. I have no wish to make demands."

Marcus stared down at the tiny hand with its roughened skin laid against the fine fabric of his coat. What a strange pair they were, the orphan and the disfigured lord. He glanced up, seeing the soft light in her wide eyes. A gentle child, he mused, a giver of comfort, softness. It was a wonder she had survived the voracious Carrs. Yet she had. There had to be strength in her somewhere. Thinking about the Carrs brought something to mind.

"I want to talk to you."

Catherine sat up a little straighter, her body suddenly tense.

Sliding his arm free of her hand, he lit another cheroot before he spoke. "I realize none of this has been easy for you, and there will be many more changes to come." He paused a moment to gather his thoughts. She was so sensitive. He wanted to be as gentle as possible. Upsetting her would accomplish nothing. "By this time tomorrow evening you will be Lady Barrington. With our marriage, you will inherit many responsibilities, but more importantly, you will no longer be dependent on Lady Carr's dubious generosity. In short you will be able to please yourself—within reason. You won't find me demanding, I assure you. To the eyes of the world, I insist we present a united, harmonious image, but what we do in private is our own affair."

Catherine nodded mutely, well able to appreciate what he was saying. She understood perfectly his desire to have society believe theirs was a normal alliance. Barbara had hurt him deeply, both his heart and his pride. She suspected that part of the reason he was willing to help her had to do with revenging himself on his lost love. How better than by bestowing on the despised cousin that which Barbara had tossed aside?

"You spoke of responsibilities..." she murmured quickly, pushing out the hurtful knowledge of what she meant to him with the practical aspects of her situation.

Marcus shrugged slightly. "I did. It amounts to very little, truth to tell. You will be required to manage Barrington Court and this house, attend whatever functions I consider appropriate. For the most part we shall remain in the country. I have lost my taste for town living, so the task should be quite simple," he added with imperfectly concealed bitterness.

Catherine noted his tone but made no comment upon it, feeling he would not wish her sympathy. "I know little of such things," she began, being inherently truthful.

"You needn't look so stricken," he murmured as he stubbed out his cheroot. "There is an excellent housekeeper. All you need do is approve the day's menus and tell her if you require anything special. Later, if you wish, you make take over any duties you feel you would enjoy. As for the rest, I shall be at your side. Once you are outfitted to your new station, you will be more at home, I assure you. I have sent instructions to the modiste for an entire wardrobe to be conveyed to us as soon as possible."

"You make it sound so simple," she said shyly, beginning to feel comfortable with him.

"It is. I shall never lie to you. I value honesty too much." Marcus got up and came round the table to her side.

Catherine tipped her head back to look at him as he towered over her. If only he loved her, it truly would be as simple as he said. She wouldn't know this urgency to make him proud of her, to win his approval. If he saw her with the eyes of love, she would be secure in his presence instead of constantly questioning each facet of their future. But there was no such emotion on his part, only her own intense feelings. She must be grateful for what she did have. Perhaps one day he would come to care for her just a little.

"I'm grateful for what you have done for me. I shall do my utmost to be a good wife. You have my promise."

Marcus read the thankfulness in her eyes. So he had come to this. The only emotion he aroused in even this insignificant female was gratitude.

"As long as you are more honest than your cousin, I shall be happy," he responded curtly, remembering Barbara's treachery. "Let us go. We have a long distance to travel." He barely glanced at her to see if she was coming as he made his way to the dressing room for his coat.

Catherine followed him silently. Would the rest of their days together always be like this? Would she so easily destroy his good moods with ill-advised words? She prayed not. She wanted more than anything in the world to make him happy again, to smooth away those bitter lines of cynicism and pain marring his face. Barbara had a great deal to answer for.

Catherine did not know when she realized she loved Marcus, but she knew she did. The feeling seemed to have grown inside her since the first time she had seen him. Then, being near him was an unattainable dream. Now her fantasy was soon to become a reality. If he but knew it, she would follow him anywhere and not count the cost to herself.

She grabbed the dark cloak Bates had found for her from the end of the bed before she hurried after Marcus. Perhaps one day, if she were very fortunate, she would walk beside him as a true wife.

# CHAPTER SEVEN

CATHARINE STIRRED DROWSILY as a door clicked open. She opened her eyes just as a rosy-cheeked face peeped in. "Good morning, miss. I'm sorry to disturb you, but my lord said it is almost time for the ceremony." Easing through the door, she carried the breakfast tray to the bed and placed it on the small table nearby. "See, I've brought you a tray, and as soon as you've eaten, I shall help you dress."

Catherine struggled to clear her groggy senses. The last thing she recalled was the long ride in the earl's—no, she must call him Marcus—carriage while he outlined his plans for the next few weeks. How had she come to be in bed and in a nightgown? she wondered uneasily. She searched her memory, coming up with a vague recollection of floating through dark halls followed by many painted eyes. The touch of gentle hands, soft murmurs, then nothing. Suddenly realizing the girl still stood awaiting orders, Catherine asked the first thing that came to mind.

"What is your name?"

The girl's anxious face cleared as if by magic, delighted at her mistress's interest. "Mary Rose, miss.

I am to be your personal maid," she stated with pride.

Catherine smiled gently, feeling better at the thought of having a young girl with a happy smile to attend her. Although she had given no thought to having a personal maid, she knew that frequently lady's maids could be veritable dragons.

"I'm glad. I've never had a maid of my own before," she confessed on impulse, deciding an open admission was better by far than pretence. She doubted her ability to keep up a pretence had she decided on such folly.

Mary Rose grinned, not at all disturbed by this information. "Don't worry, miss. His lordship told us about your guardian." She bent to prop the pillows behind Catherine's head, thereby missing her mistress's puzzled look. Then she placed the silver tray across Catherine's lap.

"Will that be all, miss?" she asked as she removed the covers.

Catherine surveyed the food and laughed softly. "Indeed, yes."

"Then shall I draw your bath."

Catherine leaned back, thinking how much her life had changed in a short day. The sun was pouring in the windows, painting shadows of gold on the floor. The birds were singing to the flowers waving in the breeze somewhere close by. She had plenty of food to eat, a lovely bed in which to sleep as long as she liked. All but her most important dream had come true in the strangest possible way.

"Oh, Mama, I wish you could be with me today," she whispered. "I have done my best to be happy with my lot. Now I plunge into a future which is both frightening and exciting. I wish you could be beside me lending me your wise counsel. If you can from where you are, help Marcus to love me just a little." She held her wish in her heart, a secret, the best dream of all. Then she smiled and opened her eyes to her breakfast, her new quarters and her new life.

The tantalizing aroma of hot tea piqued her appetite. She had never felt so cossetted, she decided, as she took a tentative sip from her cup. While she leisurely consumed the dainty pastries, she took the opportunity to study her suite.

Barrington Court was obviously very old. Her bedroom was of immense proportions and yet it was curiously homey and cozy, as though the previous generations had loved it very much. Her bed, large enough to sleep six comfortably, had a deep green canopy hung over four posters, luxurious protection against any drafts. The dark oak floor was covered with what could only be a priceless antique carpet— cream scattered with pink roses. Her gaze swept the rest of the room and landed on the exquisite white dress on a stand in one corner. Her wedding dress! She caught her breath at the fine detail and workmanship in the fairylike gown. No wonder Marcus's voice had held such reverence when he spoke of his desire for her to wear it. How beautiful his mother must have been. She knew without being told how much Marcus missed his parents.

During their long drive from London, he had spoken of his home and his life there. Most of the first part of the journey had consisted of his plans, starting with the wedding, which was due to take place in a few short hours in the family chapel. His suggestion, no command, she wear his mother's dress—his mother, he said, had been small and dainty like Catherine—had come as a complete surprise. If she had thought about it at all, which sadly she had not, she would have assumed she would be wed in the gown he had bought her in London.

Catherine replaced her empty cup and laid the tray aside. Slipping out of bed, she went to the window. She was curious about her new home. The countryside was lush and green. The land silent, at peace. If only Marcus could see his world as she did. But he was still bitter, hurt too deeply by Barbara. It was all too easy to recall the earl's comment when she had asked him what his people would say when they discovered who he would take to wife.

"They're expecting a Carr for a bride so we are giving them one. They won't be disappointed."

"Miss Catherine."

At the sound of the maid's voice, Catherine swung around, her thoughts scattering like leaves in the wind. "Yes?"

"Your bath is prepared," the maid murmured, gesturing toward the door which led to the dressing room.

"Is it time?" A shiver chased down her spine but she ignored it. She had come too far to turn back.

Mary Rose nodded, smiling.

For the next two hours, Catherine submitted to the ministrations of the excited girl. First, there was the luxury of a scented bath before a blazing fire, then her hair was washed, dried and brushed until it shone a deep, glorious red. Finally she slipped on the exquisite silk underthings before donning her wedding gown. Throughout the preparations, Mary Rose regaled her with tales of previous Barrington brides and the traditions surrounding their marriages. At least in one respect, hers was perfect. All her predecessors, with one exception, had been united in the family chapel. Knowing that stilled some of her doubts. If Marcus cared enough to carry on with tradition, perhaps in time he might come to have affection for her. It was the hope to which she clung as she stood before the long glass, while Mary adjusted the delicate lace veil over her curls.

"Oh, miss! You're beautiful!" the girl breathed in awe.

Catherine stared at her image, scarcely daring to believe her eyes. Was that really her? She raised a slender hand to touch the daringly low-cut neckline of her gown. The dress, with the exception of the waist which needed a tuck, fit her like a dream, the dull ivory satin a perfect complement to her alabaster skin. The style made the most of her slight figure, the nipped-in waist so narrow it could be spanned by two hands. The skirt cascaded to the floor in row after row of frothy satin and cobweb lace.

The short veil seemed to add to her height and crown her curls like a halo. The dark emerald pools of her eyes and the cloud of auburn hair were never so pretty or soft. Catherine barely heard the knock on the door as she stared at the vision she had become. Traces of herself lingered. Her skin was not as soft and as smooth as it could be with proper care. She had far too many bones where there should be curves. And yet...

Mary Rose appeared at her shoulder to place a spray of cream roses and lilies in her arms. "His lordship is waiting in the chapel. He sent you this."

Catherine raised the blooms to her face, inhaling their rich scent. Her first flowers. A kind gesture from a man she scarcely knew. Every touch, every gesture conveyed an outward show of emotion, but she knew it was only a show to fool the world. May she have the strength to carry it through, she prayed silently. May she bring something to this misfit marriage and to her troubled husband.

Catherine lifted her head. "It is time," she said softly. Very slowly she made her way to the door with Mary Rose trailing behind, breathing accolades to her beauty.

The earl was waiting for her just inside the family chapel, remote and distinguished in a dark grey coat and lighter breeches. He stood so tall and straight, his face solemn in the dim alcove. What was he thinking? she wondered, as she placed her hand on his outstretched arm. Was he picturing Barbara? Was he regretting his decision?

As they moved down the aisle of the empty chapel, Catherine fastened her eyes on the minister and the flower-decked altar behind him. She would not think of Barbara. That way lay only pain and fear. Once she was married to Marcus, she, and only she, could make his life complete. Maybe she didn't have his love, perhaps she never would, but she could provide an atmosphere of peace and tranquillity in his home. These were the things she must remember and strive to attain for both their sakes.

The ceremony began, the ancient ritual which would join them together "till death do us part." The beauty of the words moved her, seeming to confirm her resolution. Marcus made his responses in firm tones, very precise and clear. Though she strained to detect any note of hesitation, Catherine could find none. Somehow it appeared a good omen for the future. When it came her turn, she, too, spoke her vows without faltering. Then it was over. Her husband turned and embraced her shoulders lightly. Black eyes searched green before he lowered his head and brushed her cool lips.

His breath was warm against her mouth, his touch gentle. Catherine was unprepared for the strange yearning she experienced when he drew away. Though she had acknowledged her love to herself it had been in a purely abstract way. Her reaction to his slight caress shocked her.

She walked beside him almost blindly, trying to solve this new problem. She knew little of men and had only a vague understanding of what being married truly meant once one left the drawing room. Did he mean for them to be truly married? He had not said. Could she share the marriage bed knowing how he felt about Barbara and about herself? Would her loving him be enough? She was exhausted. That was it. It was only her weakened state which made her respond as she did.

"Are you weary?" Marcus asked, guiding her across the marble hall. "If you are, say so. Remember, you are mistress here now and bow to no one's wishes but my own."

One part of her did wish to retire. She lifted her head to stare into his eyes. But she could not. Not before him would she be a coward. Not for herself would she run. "No, I was thinking only." She tried a small smile. He didn't return it, but nor did he continue to look so grim. "The ceremony was lovely. Thank you."

Marcus gazed at her earnest face, surprised at the change a day in his care had made. She was a taking little thing, he decided, noticing for the first time how deep and warm her eyes were. Without thought, he touched her cheek gently. "A girl only marries once. Although by necessity ours was rushed, it was only fair it should be as pretty as possible," he murmured, prompted by some unknown impulse. "I hope you liked the flowers."

Catherine's smile widened. "Yes, I love them. When spring came, Mother and I would always fill the house with blooms. They were lovely, just like sunshine after the rain."

Marcus studied her intently, drawn by her sweetness, her gentleness. "No, it is you who are lovely," he said, scarcely aware he had spoken aloud. He recalled how trustingly she had nestled in his arms as he had carried her, asleep, from the carriage to her bed. The memory of the warmth of her slight body against his lingered, surprising him. "Even more so when you are asleep."

Catherine's eyes widened in surprise. She felt a blush stealing into her cheeks. So it had been he who had put her to bed. "I'm sorry I was a burden to you," she muttered, embarrassed. She stepped back a pace, not knowing where to look. What must he think of her! It seemed all he had done since they had met was take care of her needs.

Marcus felt her withdrawal immediately. For a fleeting moment, he had forgotten how he must appear to a young girl such as she. He cursed himself for a fool for not remembering the lesson Barbara had so cruelly taught. Without thought, his fingers sought and found the puckered scar. He traced it bitterly. "Don't worry, nothing happened," he assured her harshly.

Catherine saw the change in his expression with dismay. She watched helplessly as he stroked the disfigurement. "You mistake my meaning!" she cried.

"Leave it, my lady." He opened the door to the dining room with a snap. "Shall we dine?"

Catherine shook her head in defeat. There was nothing she could say which would convince him how wrong he was about her feelings. Barbara had done her work well. For a moment Catherine could almost find it in her heart to hate her cousin. Would she always live in her shadow? she wondered as she preceded Marcus through the door.

Without doubt the wedding dinner was a far cry from anything Catherine could have ever imagined. Although the kitchen staff had exerted themselves handsomely, nothing eased the tension and discord which existed in the great room.

Marcus ate little, yet the footman was called upon constantly to refill his wineglass. For the most part, he sat in brooding silence resisting all Catherine's feeble attempts to converse. Catherine tried in vain to do justice to the elaborate feast. Finally she lay down her fork, tears clogging her throat, making even token bites impossible. She stared at her plate, willing herself not to cry. She dared not lift her head, for she could feel Marcus's ebony gaze burning through her.

"Is the food not to your liking, my lady?" he asked sardonically, attempting but not succeeding in masking his temper.

Mutely she shook her head.

"Eat, then. You are far too skinny as it is," he commanded, knowing he was hurting her but unable to stop himself. He picked up his full glass and tossed the contents off in one gulp. His bride! Ha! She looked and acted terrified of him, foolish chit.

With tears threatening, Catherine needed an escape, a hiding place. "May I please return to my chamber, my lord?" she requested desperately, striving to control her quivering voice. "I am still very tired," she added for good measure.

Her husband's black scowl deepened. He did not know which of them disgusted him the most. Catherine for her meekness, or himself for the rage tearing at his soul. "As you wish."

With more haste than courtesy, Catherine quickly made good her escape.

Marcus glared at her retreating back. My bride! He saluted her with an upraised glass. Was there ever such a wedding night? He must have been mad to saddle himself with a wife. Barbara, London, the whispers and glances of pity and disgust. So far away. So unimportant here, now. His pride. Gone. In the dust. Did that matter? He was a fool. He should have come home to Barrington Court instead of nursing his wounds in the city. He would have been alone among friends, not saddled to a girl who abhorred his touch. His lips twisted into a grim parody of a smile.

He stared moodily into his glass. What was there about the chit that drew him? At present she was little more than a half-starved child, certainly not a beauty. Perhaps that was the attraction, yet it did not explain why her distaste should bother him. Why should he care what she felt? He knew he was no prize, but he would be damned if he would spend the rest of his life hiding because his wife found his battle wounds unnerving. Why hadn't he taken more notice of her withdrawal before?

He drained his wine once again. As the footman refilled his glass, he waved him aside. "Leave the decanter. I shall not require you further."

The man bowed and withdrew. Marcus picked up the full bottle. He could visit her room. He considered the thought, then thrust it away. He wanted no unwilling body in his bed. Bottle and glass in hand, he got to his feet. The night was long, as he knew to his cost. He had to have something to occupy his time. Sleep rarely came before dawn these days.

"Sleep well, my lady," he drawled as he paused at the foot of the stairs, staring up into the shadows that hid her door.

## CHAPTER EIGHT

"GOOD MORNING, M'LADY!" said Mary Rose as she entered the bedchamber.

Catherine was at the window, and she turned, smiling at the maid. Every morning for the past two weeks she had been greeted in almost precisely the same way, yet it still filled her with surprise. Mary Rose placed her usual tray of sweet chocolate and pastries on her lap when she returned to her bed. While she enjoyed the light repast, Mary Rose bustled about preparing one of her new London morning gowns. When Catherine finished, she bathed and dressed. The house was quiet as she slowly descended the stairs. Marcus was always out and about the estate by this hour. Each evening over dinner, he would tell her of his activities and enquire about her own pursuits. True to his word, he asked little of her. Nevertheless, she was determined to learn and learn quickly exactly how to be the best wife she could. She wanted no more repeats of their wedding night. She had been in agony for days after, trying to be natural yet careful not to make demands on his feelings or his time. She need not have worried, for he had treated her as more than a guest and less than a friend, never overstepping some invisible barrier only he could see. She had become accustomed to his distant mood and occasional faint smile. He talked to her of nothing of import and yet he did not show by word or deed he thought her lacking in sense. Theirs was a strange existence and one she was determined to change. She could not be a wife if he did not let her close. She might not know much of what went on in a marriage, but she did know that.

To this end, she had formed a plan, the first step of which was taken and the second already begun. She had most of her strength back, thanks to proper food and rest, and had taken her place at the head of the household with her able ally Mrs. Beall. Whether the alliance was due to intense family loyalty or to Catherine herself, she could not tell, but the older woman had responded to her willingness to be taught with sympathy and kindness. Gradually, Catherine had lost her awe of the vast old house and had begun to know and appreciate its long history. As for the more practical matters of running the great establishment, here, too, she gained skill. Her gentle manners and breeding had won the hearts of the staff from the first, a fact of which she was only vaguely aware, having attributed their willingness to help as a sign of devotion to Marcus.

Sighing deeply, Catherine entered the small sitting room and sat down at the satinwood desk where she held her morning conferences with Mrs. Beall.

How changed her life was in such a short time. Here at Barrington, her dreary existence at her aunt's house seemed a world away. Even Marcus cossetted her, though he was so correct and impersonal that perhaps managed was a better word. Had she eaten breakfast? Lunch? Was she doing too much? Had she taken her afternoon rest? She could not fault his concern, but once, just once, she wished he could see her as a woman, as his wife, instead of the exhausted girl he had rescued.

His image sprang vividly to her mind. Each day she had come to appreciate him more. His unfailing courtesy and kindness to those who served him, his dedication to his obligations and understanding for those in need. How fortunate she would be if theirs was a real marriage.

"My lady?"

Catherine looked up and forced a smile of welcome. "Come in, Mrs. Beall. I was woolgathering, I fear."

"It is the day for it," the older woman agreed before laying the day's menus on the desk for Catherine's approval. "The weather has been perfect since his lordship returned. A good omen, surely."

"Perhaps." She picked up the paper and scanned it carefully. She was in sore need of all the divine intervention she could obtain, Catherine thought silently.

After her conference with the housekeeper, Catherine went for a walk in the woods. One of the first things she had done when she had finally got her bearings was explore the park grounds. Each day she had found something new to delight her, as well as a certain peace, so necessary for life with Marcus. It was here, not in her husband's arms, that she poured out her frustrations. Finding a convenient flat stone, Catherine sat down beside the stream which formed the northern boundary of the grounds.

What did one do to attract the attention of one's husband? she wondered. If she were to succeed in the second part of her plan she had to think. If she knew more about Barrington, she could discuss some of his problems with him, or if she'd moved in his circle in London, they would have had that in common. What could she do? She desperately needed them to have a mutual interest, something to bridge the gap of distant courtesy which now existed.

A muted roll of thunder drew her eyes skyward. She frowned as she surveyed the dark clouds. She scrambled to her feet as a jagged streak of lightning lit the heavens to the west. Marcus would be angry if she got wet or chilled, she knew. For all his impersonal attitude, she did not doubt his concern for her health. He had appointed himself as a sort of guardian and he took his responsibility seriously.

Thinking of him reminded her of his destination this day. If she judged aright, he was directly in the path of the storm. She hoped he had taken shelter, for already she could feel the heaviness in the air as she hurried back to the house. It had not been long enough since he had been ill himself for a drenching to be easily ignored. Added to that was his shoulder, which she was sure still gave him pain, though whether because of the pace he set himself or the slow healing, she was uncertain.

Catherine reached the outer edges of the rose garden as the first heavy splatters hit the grass. Breathless and decidedly damp, she hurried through the side door and almost knocked Mary Rose over.

"Oh, my lady, I was just coming to fetch you," the girl explained, throwing the thick plaid cloak she carried about Catherine's shoulders. She urged her mistress up the stairs. "Your bath is being prepared right now."

Catherine smiled at the anxiety in her voice. "How good you are to me," she murmured gratefully, feeling the chill right through to her bones. She thought again how pleasant it was to have someone care for her comfort. Whatever else her marriage lacked, it did provide her with a security and haven where her feelings were important.

Late afternoon brought no lessening in the deluge pouring from the angry heavens. Catherine stood silhouetted in the drawing-room window looking out over the storm-darkened countryside. It was almost supper and there was still no sign of Marcus, nor any word. Worried, Catherine prayed he had found a place to stay. She studied the sky, frowning at the unabated tempest. She was too caught up in her thoughts to hear the murmur of voices in the hall or the door opening to admit the source of her concern. Marcus halted, dripping, just inside the room. He had intended to go straight to his chamber, but when he was met with the intelligence from his butler of his wife's fears, he had changed his mind. He watched her for a moment, noticing the slender fingers clutch the velvet draperies, the silent tense vigil she kept. Did his safety mean so much to her, or was it for herself she was concerned? Afraid of being left alone again to face the world? Surely she knew he would not leave her unprovided for. Or did she?

Catherine sensed another presence and turned, her eyes wide with fear. Relief surged through her as she stared at him. "Oh, my lord," she cried, forgetting everything in her need to assure herself he had taken no harm, "I was so worried!"

Marcus caught her outstretched hands before she could touch him. "Be careful, Catherine, I am soaking," he warned, holding her firmly away from him. "I came only to assure you I had not melted in the rain."

Catherine had to curb the urge to throw herself into his arms. She was appalled at her behaviour. She gazed at the floor as she sought to control herself. Hadn't he made it clear what he expected of her? "Forgive me," she murmured contritely. "I am delaying you."

The earl surveyed her bent head. How subdued and polite she sounded, exactly as she had all week. Suddenly he found himself dissatisfied with the change. Whatever her reason for being concerned for him, it was pleasant to find someone, besides a member of his staff, who did. He slipped a gentle hand under her chin and raised her face so that he could see her eyes, which were hidden behind a screen of absurdly long dark lashes. "Thank you, my dear, for worrying," he said softly. Then unable to resist the impulse, he lowered his head and lightly brushed her lips with his.

Catherine felt his touch, delicate as butterfly wings against her mouth. She opened her eyes to gaze at him in wonder, surprised at his tender expression. He had called her "my dear," not Catherine. Did he realize it, or was it a slip of the tongue, a meaningless phrase?

For a moment their gazes met, each searching, reaching out to the other. How long they stood together, Catherine knew not. It could have been minutes or only seconds. Water dripping from his dark hair fell on their clasped hands, breaking the spell. Both looked down at the drops of moisture.

"I'd best go—"

"You should get out of those—"

They started to speak simultaneously, then stopped. Marcus grinned, suddenly looking years younger. Catherine smiled, a wave of pleasure washing over her at the first unguarded reaction he had shown her.

"It will not take me long," he murmured, withdrawing his hands. "Will you wait?"

To Catherine his question held a promise for the future and she grasped it eagerly. "Of course, Marcus," she answered, shy and hopeful at once.

He gazed at her a moment longer before, with a nod, he turned and left the room.

Catherine returned to her position at the window. The angry sky no longer frightened her. Instead it reminded her of the turbulent depths of Marcus's eyes. The storm was passing both outside and in. She knew it as surely as she felt the weakening of the pouring rain.

In less than half an hour Marcus, freshly attired in dark burgundy coat and grey breeches, his hair still damp from his soaking, joined her at the window. His shoulder brushed hers although he made no effort to touch her. His gaze was focused on the now softly falling rain. Catherine glanced at him, admiring the clean profile, the strength of his jaw. How she loved this stranger she'd married but did not yet understand. She longed to share his dreams, his hopes, and comfort him in his disappointments.

He looked down at her as though aware of her gaze. "It is passing," he observed, watching the play of expression across her face. Somehow his words seemed prophetic. The pain and betrayal of the war and Barbara's rejection no longer pierced his soul. He had ridden long miles these past few weeks sorting through his life, tasting the bitter and the sweet. He was not ready to resume his town existence, perhaps never would be. But he was prepared to go forward. He wondered now, looking at Catherine, if she, too, had found Barrington Court a place of healing.

"Dinner is served, my lord," the butler announced from the open doorway.

Marcus extended his arm. "Shall we go in, my dear?"

Catherine placed her hand over his, warmth flooding her heart at the gentle look in his eyes. "Yes, I am starving," she teased lightly.

Neither Marcus nor his bride knew exactly what to say once they faced each other across the width of the table. The tentative response they had found was too new, too uncertain to make discourse between them easy. During the first courses their conversation was composed mainly of polite small talk. Finally Marcus could stand the strain no longer. With each successive minute Catherine had become more withdrawn. He could feel her slipping away, and he viewed the prospect with much displeasure. He did not understand his sudden need to get close to his wife after all but shunning her company, but now he wanted to give in to the urge. But how to begin? Swallowing his wine with one gulp, he signalled the footman to refill his glass. Egad, it was damnably hot and he had a raging thirst. He stared at his bride through fever-bright eyes. He did not wish to spend the rest of his days with a polite shadow, he decided in sudden irritation.

"Are you feverish, my lord?" Catherine asked, watching him. The flush on his cheeks worried her, as did his lack of appetite.

Marcus's temper was appeased somewhat by her concern. So soft, sweet, really very pretty, he decided, pleased his quixotic impulse had yielded a fitting bride. Her auburn hair burned with a deep fire in the candlelight, her eyes luminous green pools clearly mirroring her every thought. Even the gown she wore emphasized her elusive beauty. Made of sea-mist green, it clung to the creamy perfection of her small breasts, stirring the desire within him to life. Surprised that he would want her, he looked closer. Did she want him?

"My lord? Marcus?" Catherine leaned forward, worry adding a husky fullness to her voice, a seductive quality of which she was quite unaware.

Marcus came to himself with a start, knowing he had been staring. "No, I am not feverish. But I am tired. I believe I shall retire." He rose, conscious of the dull throb in his left shoulder. "Have you finished?"

Catherine nodded, certain something was wrong. She did not miss the stiff way he stood. Obviously he was in some pain, and equally clear, he did not wish her to know. She placed her hand on his arm.

"I, too, shall have an early night," she said reluctantly.

"As you wish," he said, preferring that she not look at him just so. He was having difficulty enough remembering that there were certain things a gentlemen did not do with his wife. He escorted her up the stairs to her door. "Pleasant dreams, my dear."

Catherine reached for the handle, but her eyes did not leave his face. She wanted desperately to offer comfort. Her pleading gaze was more eloquent than she knew.

Drawn to her, Marcus gave in to the irresistible need to touch her. His fingers feathered briefly over her cheek. She must care a little, this chit he married. She was too open and too honest to pretend so well.

"It is kind of you to be concerned, but there is no need. I took no harm," he assured her.

Kind? Was that what he thought she was being? When she ached to be so much more to him? "Good night, my lord. Sleep well," she whispered before she slipped hurriedly through the door. She had to escape before she blurted out her desire. How long before she betrayed herself? she wondered.

Outside, Marcus viewed the closed door with confusion. What was it about that tiny slip of a girl which touched him so? he wondered as he submitted to the ritual of changing for bed. It was not her beauty, for Barbara was by far more exquisite. Yet when he was near Catherine, he sensed a peace, a serenity which eased his mind and his aching body. Her gentleness and soft voice had made friends even of the most disagreeable of his staff. He fell asleep with the question of his growing interest still unsettled.

"HOLD THAT LINE, MEN! Fill in those gaps! They can't last much longer!"

Catherine awoke abruptly, sitting up in the darkness, bewildered by the silence. Surely that was her husband's voice she had heard. She stared in the direction of his room, searching for the shaft of light which indicated his nocturnal restlessness. The absence of illumination was unusual. She frowned at the surety growing within her that all was not well. Suddenly she caught the faint sound of a voice. It grew louder until the words were clearly audible through the closed connecting door.

"Forward men! Sabers! Push 'em back!"

Scarcely realizing her actions, Catherine slid from the bed and grabbed her robe, pulling it on as she sped to him. She neither looked for her slippers nor hesitated more than a fraction of a second at the barrier between their rooms. All was forgotten in her concern for Marcus.

The wild mutterings had ceased when she reached his side, but his bed bore evidence of disturbed slumber. The pillows lay in scattered confusion on the floor, obviously flung there by angry hands. The silken sheets were hopelessly tangled about Marcus's tossing body. Marcus himself was asleep, his hair damp against his flushed brow.

Catherine stood helplessly by, undecided whether to wake him or carefully try to make him more comfortable before she rang for Bates. She reached out a tentative hand to smooth the dark strands from his forehead and to feel for herself how high was the fever she suspected. The cool skin beneath her fingers resolved her uncertainty. It was only a nightmare, not the dreaded fever. She stroked his skin, wanting to comfort and ease his restlessness. When he quieted beneath her touch she knew a deep feeling of contentment. She stood for a moment, savouring the feeling, then her innate shyness came to the fore. She could not stay, but she would not leave until she made him more comfortable by at least straightening the bed covers.

Marcus awoke, startled at the slight figure bending over him. "Who are you?" he demanded, not fully alert.

Her head was bent as she tucked the sheets in at the foot of the bed, and Catherine jumped a little at the abrupt question. Looking up, she found Marcus watching her. "'Tis I, Catherine," she whispered moving closer. "You were having a bad dream and called out. Shall I call Bates for you?"

Marcus frowned, vaguely remembering the nightmare. Catherine, taking his silence as agreement, reached for the bellpull. Marcus stopped her with a hand on her arm.

"No, I do not want him." He flung her arm away. "I do not want anyone."

"But, my lord—" she began.

"You may stay," he said with a mocking grin. "After all, you are my wife."

Catherine flinched as though she had been struck. She made to move away, but again he stopped her. Was he ill? she wondered staring into his dark eyes. The full moonlight pouring into the windows illuminated the room almost as bright as day. Licking her lips nervously, she watched him, feeling strange flickers of sensation feather along her spine. Was it fear? Or something else which brought the spreading warmth to her limbs?

Aware only of his own needs, Marcus ignored her efforts to escape. His drew her inexorably closer until her knees rested against the mattress. Still he did not speak. In slow motion he stiffly raised his left hand to touch the ribbons tied at the throat of her robe. His injury made his fingers awkward as he fumbled to undo the silky lengths. Frustrated, he dropped his hand in disgust. Suddenly he was fully awake.

"Leave girl, while you can," he muttered without releasing her.

Catherine looked into his face and knew that the time had come for her to be more than a housekeeper. She loved him. What he felt she knew not. But he wanted her. He would not ask her. His pride was too great. He would lie alone in his great bed and deny himself.

"You have my hand," she reminded him gently, not taking her eyes from his face. She almost smiled at the stunned look in his eyes.

Marcus stared at her, wanting to send her away, wanting with more intensity than he would admit for her to stay. When her hand went to her throat to untie the bow which had defeated him, he made no attempt to stop her. Nor did he even when the robe slipped from her shoulders with a silken whisper.

His gaze travelled slowly over her pale face, down the slight fullness of her breasts to her slender body, which the almost transparent silk gown did little to disguise. She was beautiful, he marvelled. Her eyes were veiled from him, her expression smooth, showing neither passion nor excitement. And still she stirred him as no other had done before. Desire quickened in his blood. Taking her free hand he pulled her gently down to join him on the bed. She had not spoken.

"Catherine, look at me," he commanded in a deep voice. A heat beat in his veins, but he would take no bridal sacrifice out of gratitude.

Catherine raised her eyes. She knew so little. Had she misread him?

"Do you realize what you are about, little one?" he asked urgently, praying she did. "Do you truly wish this?"

Fear mixed with excitement at what she sensed was to come. "I do," she said softly, wanting them both to hear her words. She felt the curious tension in Marcus relax.

Slowly, carefully, Marcus lifted his head to brush her lips. At his touch, Catherine stiffened. Yet as his mouth moved gently over hers, she lost the feeling of strangeness. Guided by an unknown instinct, she tried to copy his actions. Her innocent response brought a groan of pleasure from his lips. Marcus gathered her tightly in his arms, pressing her breasts against his bare chest. He was burning with heat, yet she felt blessedly cool against his skin. Slipping the gown from her body, he feathered kisses over her shoulders and neck. Her shivers of delight pleased him. When at last she lay pliant and naked in his arms, he feasted his eyes on her pale loveliness, which was made even lovelier by the silvery light shining through the windows.

"You're exquisite," he muttered hoarsely as he took her mouth. His lips moved urgently over the lush sweetness of hers, demanding a response to his needs. He wanted her, all of her. His wife, his lover.

# CHAPTER NINE

CATHERINE AWOKE SLOWLY, conscious of a deep feeling of happiness. She gazed around the unfamiliar room in momentary puzzlement. A heavy weight across her breasts held her captive when she tried to sit up. She touched Marcus's bronzed arm, the sudden return of the memories of their passionate lovemaking bringing a blush to her cheeks.

She turned her head carefully so as not to wake her husband. How relaxed and at peace he appeared. Free to drink her fill of him undetected, she lovingly studied the clear-cut profile, the dark lashes and the full lips, which had stirred her senses to madness. Her heart ached as her eyes rested on the scarred left cheek and shoulder. How he had suffered! So young to be hurt so badly. And those days of fever! His hopes crushed when his arm did not regain its strength.

With the bare account Bates had offered, she had pictured his last days in France. She had hoped with her knowledge to gain an understanding of the forces which drove him. In a way she had succeeded. For a moment she thought of Barbara. Marcus turned in his sleep, his arm tightening possessively around her. A faint smile touched his mouth as though his dreams were pleasant indeed. Catherine smiled, too, hugging to her heart the moments they had spent together in the darkness. This morning it did not matter to her that he might be dreaming of Barbara, for it had been her arms which held him last night. It had been she whom he had called beautiful. Her breasts had known the touch of his lips and the weight of his head as he slept. And more than all of that was the knowledge that she could give Marcus what her vain cousin could not. Love! Children! And a purpose beyond this quiet hideaway. Once she would have thought them foolish dreams, but no longer. Marcus had shown her what it was to be a woman, his woman. He may not love her but he wanted her, and she alone bore his name.

The sounds of voices in the hall reminded her of the time. Suddenly she was conscious of her nakedness. Bates would be in soon and she must be gone. Taking great care not to wake her sleeping husband, she slipped from the bed and into her gown and robe. For a moment she stood beside him, hoping that one day she would not need to hurry to her chamber for fear the servants would find them together. With a sigh, Catherine left the room just seconds before Bates entered.

Catherine leaned against the door wondering how best to go on now that affairs had changed between them. Should she dress and join her husband for breakfast? Yes, she decided with a little smile. Today she was truly married and she belonged at his side. She did not ring for Mary, preferring her solitude. Her happiness was too new for her to wish to share it. It was almost an hour later before she walked quickly down the stairs to the breakfast room. She paused outside the door to compose herself as shyness overcame her. How would she act? How would Marcus act?

Smoothing her hands over her pale pink muslin gown, she wondered briefly if she had been wise to leave her hair loose about her shoulders, caught only with a deep rose ribbon. The tread of footsteps on the stairs behind her solved her dilemma. She turned to face Marcus.

"Good morning, my lord," she offered softly, the colour coming delicately to her cheeks.

Marcus's brow lifted in amusement. "So formal?" he teased, enjoying her shyness. How tiny she was. So fragile even now after weeks of rest and good food. "You know my name, my lady. Doesn't the occasion call for more familiar greetings!"

Happiness slipped the guard from her tongue. The smile in his eyes invited her own. "That depends." She lifted her eyes, giving him a look which was a challenge.

Arrested by the flash in her eyes and the smile curving her lips, Marcus stepped closer. "On what, my lady?" The child was flirting with him, he realized, torn between amusement and intrigue.

"On whether or not I am awarded the same privilege, of course," she replied innocently.

Knowing full well she referred to his own formality, he found a way to retaliate. "I shall call you Kate," he said, giving her a look which dared her to object.

"Then you shall be Marc." She nodded once, as though testing the nickname for size.

"You are full of confidence this morn, Kate," Marcus observed, leaning closer until his lips were almost touching hers. He wanted to see how far she would go, he told himself, even though he knew in part he was lying to himself.

Catherine did not retreat. She saw the change in his eyes and understood. The day before, she knew, she would not have. "Perhaps. 'Tis better than being a hen-hearted watering pot," she teased.

"I have never said that of you." His grin widened. He had not known she could laugh at herself.

"You, sir, are a gentleman."

"Not always, my Kate."

She blushed but held her ground. She would not be routed by a flank attack. "No, 'tis true."

His smile died a little as he stared into her eyes. "Did you like it, little one?" He had to know. He had wanted her so much, that he was not certain even now he had been as careful as she deserved.

His question caught her off guard. If she had not seen the need for reassurance in his eyes she would have tried to evade answering, for it was not an easy thing to ask a woman. "I did, Marcus," she whispered, unable to give him any but the truth.

He touched her cheek, lightly stroking the smooth curve. "I am glad, wife." He grinned, this time with wicked intent. "And you shall again."

This was teasing and then some. Catherine felt she should have made an effort to act shocked or at least conjure up a maidenly blush. But, in fact, all she could do was laugh softly. "I live in hope, my lor...Marcus," she stammered gamely. She glanced sideways at him as he tucked her hand in the crook of his arm and escorted her into the breakfast room. How much younger and relaxed he looked now. The rightness of their marriage had never been more real. Love flowed through her.

Marcus caught his breath at her shining eyes and radiant loveliness. The past never seemed further away nor less important. For the first time in a long while he knew happiness. What was it about this girl he'd married? What made him want to protect her? What was this strange need to be near her? He pushed his thoughts away determinedly. For now he was content and he wanted to know nothing else.

He signalled for the footman to set another place at the table. The post and the morning paper sat beside his plate, awaiting his perusal. He glanced at both and than at his wife.

"I do not mind if you read, Marc," Catherine murmured. "And if you would not mind it, I should like a piece of the paper."

He stared at her, surprised more at the request than her offer to allow him his habit.

"Father always shared his with Mother and me. Do you mind?" she explained, as she took a seat and saw the question in his eyes.

For an answer he took two of the pages and handed them to her, then seated himself opposite her. As he had chosen at random, one contained news of the war and the other the social gossip. He started to ask for the first back, but as Catherine was already scanning it, such action would have been churlish. Fascinated at her intent expression he forgot his own reading as he watched her. No other woman of his acquaintance would have been interested in the battle reports.

"One would think that Frenchman has information he should not," Catherine muttered, upon discovering yet another defeat of the English forces by Napoleon.

Marcus's brows climbed at the remark. "You follow the war?"

Catherine looked up at his tone. "I should not?" Had she blundered? "Father would have it that a person should be aware of what goes on in the world outside his door."

"Most women are more interested in gowns and balls and such."

Catherine glanced down at the paper she held. It had been a luxury to read the news and have all the wonders of the vast Barrington library at her fingertips these past few weeks. She had not thought that perhaps Marcus would not like her bookishness. Assuming this to be the case, she picked up the sheet she had been reading and extended it to him.

"It was not my intent to do something you could not like," she said honestly.

Marcus barely glanced at the paper. "I did not say that. I simply remarked your interest surprised me. In truth, your father had the right of it. More men and women should be concerned about Napoleon. After all, only a narrow strip of water separates us from France."

"You do not think he will seek to conquer England?"

"Who can tell what is in the mind of that one. Is he madman or genius? I know not."

"I do not think him mad enough to leave his own continent," Catherine was bold enough to suggest.

"I am not so certain." Marcus frowned, struck by the strangeness of discussing the war with his bride.

"Why?" Catherine was not about to lose the thread of the conversation. She had dreamed of such a moment as this.

"There are those in England who seek to support him. Encourage his plunder and assist him as openly as they dare. Traitors are not uncommon."

"Traitors?" Catherine's eyes widened, not having heard it put so boldly. "Who are they?"

"I am not in a position to know."

"Could you be?" The words slipped out before she thought.

Marcus opened his lips, then paused. The idea had not occurred to him, but now that it was voiced he considered the possibility. "If I chose, perhaps," he answered slowly.

Catherine understood what he did not say. The treatment he had received because of his scars had made him wary. To lend his aid in the war effort would require his returning to London and to the people who had hurt him. Only the fact she was now his wife in truth gave her the courage to reach across the table and touch his hand where it lay clenched beside his plate.

"Do you wish to hide in the country forever? I am not wise in these matters but I have read much. I learned of your courage and wisdom on the field of battle. Can you turn your back when there is something you might do?"

Marcus stiffened, anger filling him at the ease with which she spoke. Pulling his hand from hers, he glared at her. "You don't know what you are talking about. I am well out of London. And more than that, what do I know of catching spies, assuming of course that a cripple would be of use?" He rose from the table, nearly toppling his chair with his haste. "I had thought you different from the rest of your fair sisters. I had thought you would be content here and not pine for the pleasure of London. I was wrong.

But it is of no importance. Here is where we are and here is where we shall stay."

Frozen in place by the pain in his last comment, Catherine almost let him go. She loved him, she reminded herself as she watched him walk away. It did not matter to her where they lived as long as they were together. But he believed otherwise. She could not allow that belief to lie between them. Jumping to her feet, she followed him to the study. He stood at the window, his back to her, his feet braced.

"Leave me, Catherine. I have no need of you."

"You are wrong, Marcus." She faced him, more afraid then she had ever been, not of him physically but of the closeness she could be jeopardizing forever. It was so new it might not withstand this blow. "You need someone to tell you that those scars are not so very terrible. Since no one here will do so, I shall take the risk of angering you."

At that he swung around. "You, madam, have more hair than wit. You have no one. What will you do if I turn on you?"

"You will not." She clasped her hands together in front of her.

"You cannot be sure."

Pride. Marcus had more than his fair share, but there was no cruelty in him. Catherine had the measure of this man. Moving toward him, she stopped a foot away. "I am certain."

Marcus stared at her, seeing her in a new light. She stood her ground but the cost was high. "Why?"

She did not pretend to misunderstand. She, too, had pride. It had made life at the Carrs' possible. It had given her the strength to run when there was no place to run to. It would shield her now. "Because I love you." The words were soft, gentle.

Marcus experienced a mixture of fear and anger and disbelief. "You are mistaken. It is only because..." A faint flush tinged his cheeks. One did not speak so bluntly of the marriage bed and what happened there with one's wife.

She smiled then. Even in anger he treated her with respect. "I loved you before we met."

Startled, he stared at her. "It is not possible."

Catherine sat down in the chair beside her and folded her hands. For a moment she looked at her linked fingers. She had caught his interest with her declaration. Another woman would have wanted more. She was satisfied with this for now.

"I assure you it is. So many times Barbara read your letters aloud. The papers held reports of your prowess in battle. The servants spoke of you with awe and respect. I listened and learned of your honour, determination, pride and faithfulness." She raised her eyes to his. "I loved that man. But I was wrong to, for you belonged to Barbara. I tried to fight it. I did not succeed."

Marcus frowned, bewildered. Without thinking, he took the seat beside hers. "I do not love you." The words felt somehow wrong upon his tongue.

"I know."

"You accept that?"

"I have no choice. Just as you have none but to accept the scars upon your face. I could hide as you are doing now. But what use to either of us? Life moves forward with or without us. It is how we live that matters."

Marcus searched her face, seeing strength and serenity. Her words were a light at the end of a black tunnel. She was right. This woman had more courage than he. He had chosen her for a wife, thinking little of the future, but he had chosen well. "You are wise beyond your years, my Kate. You have given me a great deal to think on."

Catherine smiled gently. "Whatever you decide will be right. I know it."

"My lady?"

Catherine glanced at the housekeeper, who was hovering near the door. She had done what she could. "In a moment." She looked back at Marcus. "Will you be in for luncheon?"

"Yes," he answered distractedly. "I have some things to do. I shall be in here if you need me."

Catherine rose and left the room. As she went about her household tasks, she thought about the chance she had taken. She could not regret her stand regardless of the outcome.

THE EARL SAT LOST IN THOUGHT. He held a glass up to himself and did not like what he saw. So he was scarred. At least he was alive. Yes, Barbara's rejection had hurt, but it was not the end of the world. She had shown herself to be less than he imagined. What if he had married her and then found out her true worth?

And his wife. The stray he sheltered. What of her? Catherine had courage enough to love when there was no love in return. She faced life and remained true to herself in spite of the odds. Her clear judgment and understanding surprised him. He was indeed fortunate.

He leafed through his mail, still undecided about London. Did he want to face the stares and whispers again? Did he really know anything which might help the war effort? Would he be wanted? As his fingers toyed with an envelope, he was scarcely aware of his actions. He glanced down and noticed the seal with a start. The Carr crest. Slitting the envelope open carefully, he spread the sheets, a frown gathering as he read Lady Carr's veiled threats. Apparently, it had not taken her long to ascertain Catherine's whereabouts, and she could prove beyond a shadow of a doubt that Catherine had already been under his protection for some time before an actual marriage had taken place.

So she wanted money in return for her silence, did she? Marriage settlement indeed! She ought to be horsewhipped for what she had done to Catherine, for what she had intended to do. Suddenly his decision was made. He—they—would go to London. He would not let scandal touch Catherine. She deserved better.

He informed his wife of his decision over lunch and was surprised at her calm acceptance.

"Of course, I can be ready to travel in two days. How could I not with so many willing hands to help?" she answered calmly.

Marcus marvelled at her efficiency as he handed her into their carriage the morning of the promised date. He was more than pleased with his bride, not only for her willingness to fall in with his plans but for her ability to adapt to a life she had been drawn into with so little preparation. He was aware of the love and loyalty she commanded from his staff. Her soft voice and gentle bearing had touched the most hardened of his retainers. Her grasp of the household reins was light but skilled. A lady to her fingertips.

"You look lovely, my dear," he said, as he settled beside her in the carriage.

Catherine smiled, her gaze travelling over her serviceable green pelisse with satisfaction. "Anyone would in clothes such as these. You are a dab hand at the ordering of a lady's wardrobe," she teased, then added more seriously, "I would not wish to disgrace you."

Marcus's response was reassuringly prompt. "There is no fear of that." He reached across to take her hand, lifting it to his lips. "I am proud of you just as you are. Your naturalness is a jewel in a world filled with artifice," he murmured huskily.

Since that one night he had denied himself the pleasure of her arms, wanting to understand the love she gave so freely. Now he found that understanding held no importance if it meant staying from her side. He needed her. He wanted her smiles and her words.

"Thank you," Catherine whispered, deeply touched. She had been so afraid her response to his lovemaking or her declaration of love had prompted him to withhold himself from her. Only the fact that there had been warmth in his eyes when he looked at her, a softness in his voice when he spoke which had not been there previously, had given her hope and the patience to wait for him to reach out to her.

"Would you tell me what we shall do in London?" she asked, offering him a diversion.

Marcus had been wondering how to acquaint Catherine with Lady Carr's threat. Her question gave him the perfect opening. "Primarily, I have some business to discuss which concerns us." He noted her attentive expression and searched for the words to explain without causing her discomfort. "I am sure you are aware how irregular our actions were when we left London together."

Catherine nodded, watching him carefully, seeing the worry he was trying to hide.

"A few days ago, I received a letter from your aunt."

"What did she say?" It took little imagination to picture Barbara's and Lady Carr's rage at her marriage to the title they had sought for themselves.

He was silent for a moment recalling her aunt's arrogant words. He was glad Catherine had not seen the letter, yet it was best she be aware of the threat which awaited them in town. "There is no easy way to explain. She is furious at our marriage, more so, I think, because Barbara is still unwed. At any rate, she intends to make trouble if she can. I am not telling you this to worry you, but you need to know. It is entirely possible our return will be met with ugly rumours. You must be prepared for them, although I doubt anyone will be foolish enough to approach you directly."

"Perhaps I should have stayed at home."

"Nonsense," Marcus denied briskly. "What would that have accomplished?"

She gestured vaguely. "I do not know. My presence might only worsen the situation."

"If you do not go, then it appears as though we are not happy or that I am ashamed of you. I am certain you will agree neither idea is acceptable. We must present a united front, especially as I have decided to offer my services to the War Office." He dropped his announcement into the discussion, hoping to divert her.

Catherine's eyes widened at the news. Grasping his hands in hers, she smiled in delight. "I am so glad. You will do well, I know it. When did you decide?

Why did you not tell me?'' In her excitement, her words tumbled together.

"Just now. And I did,'' he murmured, enjoying her reaction. Her smile was the sun after the rain. Her faith was a rock a man could cling to in the stormy sea. "So you see it is quite unsuitable for you to desert me now. I shall need you to brave my wrath on occasion.'' He touched his scar, his good humour evaporating. "The world has not changed and neither have I. I will not like the whispers, and the glances which shy away. Nor the people who will try to use us both. I am no longer kind. I need you to remind me.''

He spoke not of love but need. Less by far than she hoped one day to have, but more than she'd had the day before. "I am glad you need me. For you I would face a hundred women like my aunt and Barbara.''

Marcus relaxed with a grin at her extravagant offer. "Unlikely that a hundred of such ones as they exist, my dear. Besides, let us not approach our stay with so grim a purpose. What shall we do for pleasure? Surely there are things which you would like to see and do.'' He no longer wished to think of what awaited them in London. For the moment he wanted to enjoy his wife's company without considering the past or the future.

"Everything and anything,'' Catherine replied promptly, loving his smile and giving him one of her own.

"Your wish is my command, my Kate," he teased, patting her hands. "Let us make a list. It should while away the hours, for there is much to see and do."

# CHAPTER TEN

MARCUS STOOD IN FRONT of the building which housed the Horse Guards. The early-morning sun shone over the old stone, highlighting every brick. This was his future. Catherine had been more right than she knew. If he could not fight for his country, then he would serve in other ways. Walking up the stairs he entered the almost silent corridors, passing no one he knew on his way to Sir John Waring's office. Sir John was the head of the Horse Guards and would, if he accepted Marcus's help, be his superior. A young officer was on duty at the desk. He rose when Marcus entered, asked his name and then bade him to be seated while he discovered if Sir John was free. A moment later Marcus was shown into the inner sanctum to find Sir John seated in front of a small fire, smoking a pipe. He gestured Marcus to the chair beside him.

"It took you long enough, my lord. I expected you many weeks past. I have a letter from the duke singing your praises. What kept you? We have sore need of men like you."

Marcus stared at the older man, surprised at the greeting. "I did not mention to the duke an intention to offer my services. How came he to know of them?"

"I suspect he knows you. It is sufficient for a man of his perception." Sir John shrugged slightly. "Allow me to wish you happiness on your recent marriage. I am told the Lady Catherine is a bit of a dark horse, but a lovely one."

Marcus's eyes narrowed at the reference to Catherine. "We just arrived yesterday. Your intelligence does you credit."

Sir John smiled slightly, although there was no humour in his answer. "Not always, although we try our poor best."

"You know why I am here."

"I do." He reached for a thick folder on the table beside him. He passed it to Marcus. "This is your first assignment. Tomorrow afternoon, early, another like it will be brought to your office by special courier. I hope you find the office we have selected to your liking. You see, we really were expecting you. I shall want to speak again. Be prepared."

Marcus took the report and got to his feet. He had been dismissed. Turning, he started for the door. Sir John's voice stopped him.

"There are many who know of your injuries. Many who would seek to make you feel less than you are. Pay the foolish no heed. I know. I, you see, lost a part of myself in the war."

Marcus swung around, watching as Sir John rose awkwardly to his feet. One leg had been amputated at the knee and supplanted with a wooden peg. The two men faced each other, knowledge of human cruelty in each man's eyes. With a nod, Marcus turned and left the room. No words were necessary. Feeling better about himself than he had in a long time, Marcus was shown into his office, where he sat down. For a long moment he stared out the window, thinking about the strange twists his life had taken. But for fate he could be married to Lady Barbara or perhaps still fighting the war. He would not have Catherine nor this chance to render his services yet again in a new capacity. Lady Barbara would never have encouraged him to seek a different direction. Only Catherine had seen his need. He smiled, thinking of her pleasure when he would tell her of his position.

Applying himself to the task at hand, he spent the next few hours going over intelligence on the conspiracy of spies which seemed to be centred in London. He was shocked at the extent to which the war effort was being compromised on the home front. The Horse Guards might well have taken an ad in the *Gazette* so freely did the information move. Frowning, he continued to read as the report slowly traced its way almost to the source, the leader. Finally, only the identity of the man who had put the operation together was missing. It was late when he sat back in his chair and stared out the window. No wonder battles which should have gone to the English had miraculously been won by the French. Angry, for he had been there to see the carnage, he swore long and hard before closing the report and placing it in the locked safe for the night. It was time to go home to Catherine.

"PRAY TELL ME WHAT HE SAID," Catherine demanded the moment she was alone with Marcus. She had been waiting all day in a fever of impatience.

Marcus grinned, enjoying her enthusiasm. "I shall not tell you a thing if you do not eat your dinner. You are still too thin for my liking."

Catherine wrinkled her nose at him, before applying herself to her dinner. "I shall eat as long as you talk," she promised.

Marcus picked up his wineglass, took a long swallow, then began his tale between mouthfuls of his own meal. Catherine listened intently, watching his expression change with each word. She felt like crying when he described the way Sir John had showed him his injury. She knew how the thought of being less than the man he had been disturbed Marcus. She sent up a silent prayer of gratitude for the older man's compassion.

"I am glad you decided to brave my wrath, my Kate," Marcus murmured at the end of his story. "But for you I might have dwindled into a bitter man." He lifted her hand and carried it to his lips. His eyes held hers as his tongue lightly traced the vein at her wrist. Her shiver of response pleased him. The clouds of passion in her eyes demanded and pleaded at the same time. "Have you finished? I have plans for this night, plans I think you will like very well."

Catherine read the desire in his eyes and rejoiced in its presence. She wanted to be in his arms again, held close to his heart. "I am very tired, my lord," she whispered huskily, daring to tease. With each day, she was more at ease with him.

"Then let us get you to bed, madam wife." Marcus rose, drawing her up with him. Tucking her hand in the crook of his arm, he led her from the room. Neither noticed the footman, too engrossed were they in each other.

"KATE, WHERE ARE YOU?"

Catherine dismissed the housekeeper, striving to keep the smile from her face. When Marcus was gone the sun dimmed. When he returned her world was complete. "I am here." She walked to the door of the small room which she used for household matters. Marcus strode down the hall toward her, his face clearing at the sight of her.

"Come, get your bonnet and pelisse. I have a surprise." He took her arm and linked it with his.

"Another one, my lord?" she asked, going with him willingly.

They had been in London but two days, each one bringing more changes in their lives. Marcus had been rarely at home, having spent most of his time at the War Office. This morning had seen him off on a mysterious errand.

"The first one, my appointment, was for me. This, my dear, is for you." He paused at the foot of the stairs where Mary Rose waited with Catherine's bonnet and pelisse.

"May I guess?"

"You may not." He took the ribbons of the pink hat perched on her head and tied them under her chin. Flicking a finger down her nose, he grinned wickedly. "You may close your eyes. I shall lead you if you trust me."

Catherine laughed softly. "I trust you. Do you not know that?" Her brows arched. Though he spoke not of love, she felt his affection. Her confidence grew hourly in the strength of his feelings.

"I do, sweet Kate. Now shut your eyes."

Obediently Catherine closed her eyes and let him lead her out the front door and down the steps.

"Now open."

Catherine opened her eyes and found herself staring at the most elegant carriage, drawn by a matched pair of greys, she had ever seen. "For us? I did not know we needed another."

"We do not. This is for you."

Catherine turned, searching his face. No one had ever given her such a costly gift. "You cannot mean it! I have never seen anything so beautiful."

Marcus stepped closer but did not touch her. "I wanted you to have a carriage of your own. I wanted you to be free to move about without asking me if you could go. And these are your people—Joe, the coachman, and Jem, the footman.''

Catherine nodded and smiled at the two men, then turned back to Marcus and asked, ''But why?''

He shook his head, tucked her hand in his and guided her to the carriage door. ''Let us take a ride, madam wife, and I shall endeavour to explain.'' He handed her inside.

Catherine barely noticed the soft gray squabs as she settled against the cushions. The carriage moved forward the moment Marcus was seated beside her. He took her hand, his eyes holding hers.

''I shall not always be available now that I have taken your sage advice. I do not want you to be a prisoner in our home as you were in your aunt's.''

''There is no comparison!'' Catherine hurried to say.

''Perhaps not. But I want you to be free to please yourself. I want you to enjoy our life, not find yourself shackled. So I have given you wings.'' The words hardly conveyed the feelings which he'd had on thinking of his gift. An impulse had prompted his visit to Tattersall's. The carriage had been a fortunate chance, for it had been made for another but not collected. Had he ordered it himself he could not have chosen better for his bride. ''I want you to be happy,'' he finished simply.

''But I am,'' Catherine murmured in bewilderment. ''Why would you think that I am not?''

"I do not think it." A small lie which he hoped would be forgiven. He could not explain to her his guilt at taking her love and offering her no coin in return. A carriage and pair were small recompense for all she brought to his life. "I want to see you smiling, always.'

She smiled then, beginning to understand. The feeling was one she knew herself. Hope glowed brighter than ever. The dream she had prayed for was close. "Then I shall. I shall do it so often you will wonder that there is not something amiss."

He lifted her fingers to his lips, kissing them lightly. "Never, my Kate. I shall simply consider myself the most blessed of men. I shall grow insufferably smug in the bargain."

"Impossible."

"We shall see. Now, look about you. Observe our city, for this is our first tour."

For the next hour Catherine found herself treated to a view of London she'd never before enjoyed, with Marcus as her able guide. It was nigh luncheon by the time they returned home. Marcus handed her down from the carriage, and they entered the house together, to be met by the butler with a note. Marcus took the missive, frowning at the seal. Catherine had seen too many of the Carrs' letters not to recognize this as one.

"I shall meet you in the dining room, Catherine," he murmured, heading for the study.

Catherine followed him, for once not falling in with his wishes. "It concerns me," she reminded him quietly.

Marcus looked at her, seeing her determination and realizing that he did not wish to shut her out of his life even in this way. Strange. A week ago he would not have considered involving her. "As you wish."

Neither spoke as they entered the study and sat on the settee. Marcus opened and read the letter. His frown deepened, turning to a scowl. "That woman! First she ignores the note I sent round to her and now this." He tossed the single sheet down. "She is an unprincipled fool."

"What does she say?"

"Read it for yourself. I warn you, you will not find it pleasant."

Catherine picked up the paper, remembering the life she had led at the Carrs. The contrast between then and now was the difference between sunshine and darkness. A moment later she set the note aside, prey to a confusion of emotion. Though she had no love for her aunt, she felt pity for her circumstances. There was anger, too, that Lady Carr would seek to harm Marcus through her. "She is desperate."

"So it would seem."

"What proof can she possibly have that I stayed that one night with you? Would it matter so very much?"

"It would matter a great deal. As for proof, I think that a lie. Only Bates, you and I knew. And the coachman."

"What will we do?"

"See her as she demands. If she is as desperate as she sounds, I shall do something. I cannot have her in debtors' prison, for she is kin. It would do none of us credit."

"I cannot like it. It is she and Barbara who have brought themselves to this pass. It is not fair that you should bear the burden because of me and our marriage."

"Nor can I like it, but not for that reason. I do not wish a tie with the Carrs. They have harmed you. That gains them no favour with me." His voice hardened as he remembered the way she had looked when he had taken her in. "They would have sold you into marriage to that Thatcher."

Startled at his anger, Catherine studied him closely. "You sound as if you know of him."

"I do. I made it my business to discover the cut of his coat. I do not like what I found. I think he will not prosper in the future."

"Marc, you did not do something to him." Catherine touched his hand, her eyes searching his. "You need not champion me. He can do nothing now."

"I know, but I am your protector. I will see justice done. I shall simply let the extent of his business dealings be known. The man is a cheat with a long list of bad connections. I intend to put him out of business, as he well deserves." He held her hands, caressing the delicate fingers, which no longer bore the marks of drudgery. "I told you I am not kind."

"You are to me." She swayed toward him, her love deepening with every word he spoke. No one since her parents had cared for her so much.

Marcus caught her close, her lips calling to him, her scent light as a summer breeze, reminding him of the delight of her body pressed to his. "You are my wife, my Kate. What touches you, touches me," he whispered hoarsely.

She searched his face. Each day they grew closer, more in tune with each other. "It is the same for me."

"I thank the fates that you dropped into my arms that night." He pulled her closer still until she rested in his lap. So small was she that he almost felt he held a child—until his hands smoothed over her delicate curves, the curves of a woman, his woman. "I am truly glad that it is you I wed, not Barbara." The truth slipped out without plan. He did not regret his confession when he saw the happiness on her face. "She is not and never was the woman you are. I trust you. I never expected to need that with the woman I took to wife. You are wise and brave. Those things, too, held no importance until I wed you. I need you more than I can tell you." Deep within there was regret he could not make a more impassioned declaration. His finesse was sadly lacking, and yet he could not pretend pretty phrases. He wanted her to know the truth of his heart.

Tears welled in Catherine's eyes, flowing in silver streams of happiness down her cheeks. She smiled, though her lips trembled. "I love you."

He kissed her slowly, deeply, savouring the sweetness of her mouth. Her arms around his neck were ties to the future he welcomed. Her warm body, tucked close to his, made him feel complete and whole again. His scars did not matter. Nor did gossip. Nor spies. Nor the future. Nothing was real but Catherine.

"Shall we miss luncheon, my Kate?" he whispered against her ear. Her shiver of delight brought a smile to his lips.

"In the middle of the day, my lord?" The idea should have shocked her. Instead it excited her.

"In the middle of the morning, the afternoon or the night, my lady. Choose." He nipped at her ear. "I am here to serve you."

"We cannot," she returned breathlessly. "Though I wish we could. You have your work this afternoon."

Marcus lifted his head to grin at her, his eyes alive with wickedness. "Madam wife, you shock me, I vow. I had not thought to take so long."

Catherine blushed a lovely pink as she tried to glare at him and stifle her laughter at his banter. "You are a complete hand. You should not tease me so."

"But you rise to the bait so well." He stole a kiss before she could evade him.

"I have not your experience."

"I would gladly teach you."

Catherine smoothed her skirts, keeping her expression demure and maidenly with effort. "It would be unseemly."

"It would be a pleasure."

She lifted her head, laughing. "That it would, my lord," she agreed saucily, quickly slipping off his lap and out of reach. Her glance fell on the note, her amusement dying. She gestured to the paper. "I had forgotten."

Marcus frowned. "As I." He picked up the missive and consigned it to the flames in the fireplace. "We shall see your aunt. Tomorrow, I think." He rose and tucked her hand in his. "For now let us enjoy a repast, and then I shall be off for a short time. Tonight we shall attend our first engagement. Did I tell you I met a friend at Tat's? He and his wife are giving a small soirée and we are invited. Which brings me to the third surprise, which you will find in your closet upstairs. Celeste has created a town wardrobe for you. Most of it is still to be delivered, but there is enough for a few days."

Catherine leaned against his arm, enjoying the strength and warmth pressed against her side. "Will you think me fainthearted if I admit to a small attack of the vapours at the prospect of entering the social scene?"

"I shall. Where is the woman who would brave my wrath? Do you tell me that she is frightened by a few tabbies? I think my wrath is a poor thing if that is so."

Catherine laughed, as she knew he meant her to. "It shall be on your head if I stumble or drop my soup in my lap."

"My dear. You would not ruin my consequence with such manners. I cannot have that," he drawled with mock seriousness. "Besides, I have it on the best of authority, they are not serving soup!"

MARCUS LEFT HIS TOWN HOUSE that afternoon well pleased with himself and his world. Marriage to Catherine had given him more than he thought to have. He was smiling as he sat down at his desk to begin going through the report on the spy activities in and around London. His good humour died a swift death on finding one name mentioned too frequently in the intelligence before him. Lord March. Report in hand, he left his office. A moment later he sat with Sir John.

"I see you have read our report," the older man remarked, lighting a pipe and leaning back in his chair.

They could have been two men discussing the weather for all the emotion Sir John showed. "I did. Why did you not tell me when I first spoke to you? You know Lady Barbara is seeking an attachment."

"Precisely. A most fortunate circumstance, having you approach us just when we were in need of a way to trap our man and eliminate his threat. A certain document has somehow contrived to escape our walls. We believe Robert now has the memo and is planning to pass it along, if not take it to France himself. I fear that the man assigned to watch his lordship has betrayed himself and Lord March now knows we are suspicious of him." Sir John frowned deeply, a note of restrained anger in his voice. "The man has been dismissed for his clumsiness. Unfortunately, we can not undo the harm he has done our investigation."

"How may I help? I will tell you now that my wife and I do not stand on good terms with her family."

Sir John smiled a little. "I like your honesty, my lord, but you do not need to tell me that. I know. I know, too, that Lady Catherine came to you when she left her aunt. Why, I am unsure, though it is of no import. The important issue is that you, with the help of your lady if needs be, must get close to Lord March as quickly as possible. I would have preferred a better-thought-out plan, but you are our only chance. That memo must not leave the country. Lady Barbara, we have reason to believe, is important to Lord March. It is thought he will attempt to take her with him, or failing that send for her. We expect it to be practical rather than personal, but for whatever reason, she is our link."

"Is she involved?" Marcus asked, more for Catherine's sake than caring whether Barbara was a spy.

"No. The woman is too shallow to ally herself with anything political." Sir John puffed on his pipe, watching Marcus closely.

"I do not know if can help you. I can't think that Lady Barbara or her mother will believe I seek an acquaintance."

"There is no alternative. Until you came to us we were at *point non plus*. Short of assassinating Robert, which would have raised all sorts of unpleasantness from his family and his friends and may not have saved the memo at any rate, we had no way of monitoring his moves. He is on his guard and won't be easily taken in. You will need your wits about you as it is."

Marcus stared at the report he held, considering his course. For himself he would have accepted in a moment. But he had to consider Catherine. Thinking of her, he realized he could not turn away from Sir John. She would urge him to agree if she were with him now.

"We shall do our best," he said quietly, raising his eyes to Sir John's. "There well could be a scandal because of Catherine."

Sir John smiled, not a gesture of humour, but rather the look of a fox before he raids the henhouse. "I think not. My consequence is not as great as yours, but my allies are the strongest in the land. You will not lose by this, neither you nor your lady."

"May I tell her?" The idea of keeping his activities a secret from Catherine was abhorrent.

Sir John frowned. "I do not think it necessary. It has been my experience that ladies do not keep a still tongue, nor are they good in a crisis."

"Not my Kate," Marcus disagreed firmly, thinking of the waif, dressed as a boy, dangling from the end of sheet in the middle of the night.

Sir John searched his face, seeing the strength and intelligence written there. "You think she will aid you in this?"

"I know so."

Silence. Sir John chewed his pipe. The fire in the grate popped gently. Marcus sat unmoving. "So be it. The duke speaks highly of your nerve under fire. This is a different battle we fight. You may choose your own allies and weapons. I will depend on your discretion."

CATHERINE STARED at her reflection in the glass. Mary Rose had done her job well, as had the hairdresser Marcus had insisted she engage. She had never been in such looks. The French cut of her gown showed off her slim figure to advantage, the delicate buttercup shade bringing out hidden gold highlights in her hair. Swept high in a halo of curls with a few escaping to tease her ears and neck, the style added a regal height. A diamond necklace, tiny diamond eardrops and a sprinkle of diamonds in her hair made her feel as if she were bathed in stardust. The

Barrington family ring glowed softly on her finger, proclaiming to the world that she belonged to Marcus. She smiled at her image, liking the thought.

"I like that little smile. What does it mean?"

Marcus's reflection joined hers. His black coat over biscuit-coloured breeches was a perfect contrast to her own attire. She had never seen him so handsome. The scar on his face was less vivid, from the days in the healing sun at Barrington Court, which had touched his skin with gold.

"It means that I find the world a beautiful place," she murmured, turning to face him.

"You are happy?"

"You need ask?"

He touched her cheek, his fingers trailing down her neck and across the top of the low-cut bodice of the gown. He frowned a little on seeing the amount of velvety flesh on display. While the creation was in good taste, he found he did not like the thought of others seeing her thus. But he would not spoil her pleasure. Instead a quiet word with Celeste and a yard or two of lacy shawl would be the ticket.

Catherine inhaled deeply at the caress, her lashes drifting shut as the familiar feeling of weakness invaded her limbs. He had only to touch her and she remembered the fire of his lovemaking and wished for more.

"I wish we could stay at home," he whispered.

"As I do," she confessed, swaying closer.

He kissed her once, hard, then set her from him. "Come, my Kate. Our first appearance must not begin with our being late, however tempting the desire to do so!"

## CHAPTER ELEVEN

CATHERINE ENTERED THE BALLROOM on Marcus's arm, aware of the silence which had fallen at the announcement of their names. All eyes were on them. Her fingers tightened as she fixed a small smile upon her face. She would not disgrace Marc, she promised herself. Her lineage was naught to be ashamed of.

"Be easy, Kate," Marcus whispered, bending his head close to her ear. In his need to reassure Catherine, he forgot his scar and the receptions he had received upon returning from France.

Catherine turned her head, smiling up at him. "Worried about your consequence, my lord?" she teased shakily. The effort was worth the cost when she saw the worry leave his eyes.

"To be sure, my lady," he replied.

At that moment, neither was aware that the members of the ton had given a collective gasp at the obvious affection between them, nor did they notice the presence of Lady Barbara on Lord March's arm.

"Marcus, you came." Sir Geoffrey Linchfield grinned as he made his greeting. "And Lady Catherine. My wife, Priscilla."

Lady Priscilla smiled, her grey eyes sparkling. "Quite an entrance, my dears," she murmured humorously. "You have quite made my gathering."

Catherine was uncertain how to take the lady's words, but when Marcus only laughed and teased her back she relaxed.

"We did our poor best," he agreed, glancing around the assemblage. His gaze found and rested for a moment on Lady Barbara and her escort. Anger flickered briefly in his eyes before he forced himself to betray none of his feelings. As yet he had not the chance to confide in Catherine about Lord March. "I see many whom I know here."

Sir Geoffrey followed his eyes, grimacing ever so slightly. "The invitation was given before we knew of your presence in town."

Catherine turned her head, catching the angry look that Barbara sent in her direction. It had not occurred to her that her cousin would be present. Keeping her smile firmly in place, she tried to be as composed as Marcus.

"Come, Catherine, let us dance a while," Marcus suggested, guiding Catherine down the short flight of stairs to the dance floor. The orchestra struck up a cotillion, and they joined the set just forming. The dance steps were familiar to Catherine only through watching. She had not thought to tell Marcus she could not dance. As a result she had to concentrate intently on her steps, feeling confident only when partnered by him. When the set ended she was glad to circulate among the guests, being introduced to many, quizzed by some, but ignored by none. It was more than an hour later before she and Marcus came face-to-face with Barbara.

"Hello, little cousin," Barbara drawled, glancing pointedly at the diamonds and the costly gown before her eyes rested on Catherine's face. "You do well, I see, since you left our home."

Catherine stiffened, but held her tongue. She could feel the eyes of the ton waiting for a scene. "I think marriage agrees with me," she said mildly.

Barbara's expression tightened, the reference to her own still-unwed state a slap which she had not expected. Anger blazed in her eyes. She had opened her lips to retaliate when Robert stepped into the breach.

"Temper, my pet. You have an audience," he murmured just loud enough for the three to hear. "None of us would like a scandal." He raised her hand to his lips, smiling faintly.

Barbara stared at him, torn between letting fly and giving in. 'Twas ever thus. His dark eyes held her in check and beckoned her onward at his will. She sighed, swaying slightly closer. "As you wish."

Marcus watched the interplay, worried at the influence which Lord March exercised. It appeared that Sir John had the right of the situation between

Barbara and her suitor. Why the man had not come to the point was a mystery.

"Perhaps our ladies would care to dance." Robert eyed Marcus speculatively. "Are you brave, my friend? Shall we give the tabbies something to talk about?"

"What do you suggest?" He had a feeling he knew, although he could not fathom Lord March's reasoning.

"An exchange of partners."

Catherine glanced at him quickly, having no desire to be touched by other than her husband and certainly never by Lord March. Barbara looked equally unhappy with the arrangement, though not for the same reasons.

Marcus looked at Catherine for a long moment. He wanted to tell her to trust him but could not. Whether she read his wish in his eyes, he knew not. But he did see her sigh and felt the loosening of her fingers on his arm.

"I warn you, I am sadly out of practice, I fear," Catherine said, giving his lordship her hand. She managed not to recoil when he bowed over it before leading her onto the floor. If she could just get through a few minutes she would be back at Marcus's side. Surely one dance with this man would be all her husband would ask of her.

The music began, a waltz, her first since being given permission by one of the patroness of Almack's just moments before. Lord March was an excellent dancer, had Catherine been in the mood to notice. Instead, all she could see was the way Barbara and Marcus moved in time to the music. The candlelight was kind to them both, striking sparks of gold off Barbara's hair and throwing into handsome relief the finely sculpted bones of Marcus's face.

"You need not worry about your cousin. She has no interest in your husband."

Catherine raised startled eyes to Lord March's. She did not like the man, but for an instant she found her feelings less certain. "I do not."

He smiled slightly, his gaze on his lover. "She will play. That is and always will be her way."

"You love her," Catherine stated in astonishment, too surprised to guard her tongue.

He glanced down at her. "Not as you mean, my dear lady. We are of a kind, she and I. I know her better than she knows herself. She seeks to bring me to heel with a flirtation. It will not happen."

Curious, Catherine voiced her question. "Why do you tell me, a stranger?"

"A gentle impulse, perhaps." He gave a Gallic shrug, his lips twisting.

"I do not think you are given to such things."

"Then let us say I admire courage. And I dislike excessively seeing one pay a price for loyalty."

The depth of feeling in his voice was strange. Catherine heard shades of meaning beyond the words. Puzzled, she studied the man. His dark eyes held some secret which gave him no pleasure. The music died and the dance ended before she could decide what she thought of him.

He bowed over her hand, smiling a little. "I think I owe you a belated apology, my lady. Once we met, and I acted less than a gentleman. Forgive me."

Catherine's lips parted, too astonished to reply. She had not thought he would remember, much less remark, on the occasion. Before she could say a word, Marcus appeared at her side. He handed Barbara back to March and tucked her hand into the crook of his arm.

"Shall we repair to supper, my dear?" he asked quietly, drawing her away from the pair.

Catherine glanced at him. "Marcus, I do not understand this," she whispered, smiling slightly for the benefit of those watching.

"I shall explain when we return home. For now, trust me," he said as he seated her at the small table beside the windows leading to the gardens.

He glanced across the room, watching, for a moment, Robert and Barbara. An odd pair. After seeing them together he did not know what to think. He had met Lord March only a few times in the past. What he had known of him was unexceptional, other than the man was a known flirt and well thought of by the ladies of his acquaintance. He lived high, having seemingly deep pockets. His ancestry was French on his mother's side with extensive holdings on the continent rumoured to be lost to Napoleon. His English lands were less rich. He had escaped all manner of snares tossed his way by the matchmaking mamas until Barbara had taken his fancy. Yet despite his obvious preference he had not come up to scratch. A tangle indeed.

"ARE YOU TIRED?" Marcus crossed the room to take Catherine in his arms. The loose negligee she wore was little protection for her nakedness. His hands caressed her soft curves as he drew her close, his lips brushing hers.

"A little, but more than that I am curious," she admitted, shivering in delight at the feel of his hands on her body. She pressed nearer, aching in all those special places he had taught her existed.

Marcus sighed, wishing he could put off his explanations. "You will not like it."

Catherine tipped back her head to stare at him, her desire ebbing slightly at his tone. "Is it trouble?"

"More than you can imagine."

"Barbara and Lord March?"

He nodded, before leading her to the chaise beside the window and sitting down with her in his lap. "What I shall tell you must go no farther than your ears."

"I promise." Fear touched her heart at his seriousness.

"You and I are being drawn into the heart of a spy web. It is believed at the War Office that Lord March is the leader."

Catherine inhaled sharply, her eyes wide with shock. "And Barbara?"

"An innocent, it is believed. He has a memo." Very slowly and carefully Marcus related all that he knew. "So you see we must tread warily. Sir John believes that Robert will take Barbara with him when he leaves, if he leaves. We must contrive to stay as much in the know of Barbara's activities as is possible."

"I agree, though I cannot see her or my aunt welcoming my appearance."

Marcus studied her, frowning at the certainty in her voice. "Do you think he will take her with him?"

"He as good as told me so. He called them two of a kind. In his own way I think he loves her. He spoke of loyalty, too. I cannot like the man, but I confess, he puzzles me. Had you asked me before tonight I would have said I disliked him heartily. Now I am less positive." Her brow wrinkled in thought. "Is it possible the War Office is wrong?"

"There is evidence."

"I feel sorry for my aunt. If he does succeed in spiriting Barbara away and his activities come to light, the scandal will kill her. For all her faults she is a proud woman. As is Barbara. No matter whether she goes or stays she will lose."

"It cannot be helped. Both have chosen their course."

"How shall we get close?" Catherine demanded, considering the situation. "And in such a short time?"

"Your aunt, herself, has given us the way. Tomorrow we meet with her. I shall offer to make her an allowance, in return demanding a charade of a closer relationship for the benefit of society so that the rumours circulating about us will be scotched. She will agree, for I shall make the allowance a handsome one and her needs grow greater every day and the hounds pursuing her inch nearer. Barbara will be more of a problem, but it is the best I can contrive for now. We must simply be alert. The memo must be passed on soon, or its value will be lost."

He held her tight for a moment, thinking on what might have been Catherine's fate had she not run that night. Catherine relaxed against him, her thoughts running on a similar path.

"I am glad it was you that night," she whispered softly.

"You dropped out of the window and knocked me flat. I have not recovered my balance yet."

She turned in his arms, her hands slipping to his shoulders to caress him lightly. "Are you sorry, my lord?"

He took her lips before the last word had left her mouth. Moulding her to him, he showed her in the best possible way how little he regretted her unheralded arrival in his life. The candles burned low in

the holders, the silence broken only by soft murmurs and low moans of pleasure. The dawn inched
across the sky before the silence was that of two
sleeping peacefully, entwined together so closely that
they seemed one.

MARCUS GLANCED AT CATHERINE as the butler announced the arrival of Lady Carr. He had never been
more proud of her than at this moment, for the way
she rose to greet her aunt without showing the least
sign that this was more than an ordinary social call.

Giving his attention to Lady Carr, he decided that
the past few weeks had not dealt well with her. The
majestic figure was swathed in purple and black, a
hat too young for her advanced years perched atop
a mass of dyed-brown curls. Her hawklike face was
arranged in a civil expression, belying the watchful
look in her eyes. He made his greeting, then gestured her to a seat.

"I am glad to see that you have come to your
senses," Lady Carr announced, firing the first salvo.

Catherine sat back, allowing Marcus to handle the
interview as they had decided. By rights there was no
reason that she need be present, save for the fact she
wanted to share the trouble her marriage had brought
to Marcus. But for her, he could have pursued Lord
March in a different, perhaps more effective manner.

"I received your letters, if that is what you mean," he countered coolly. He paused then added, "I consigned them to the fire where they belonged."

Lady Carr dropped her milder demeanour to glare at him. "You fool."

"I think not. Neither of us wish a scandal." Again he paused, letting her dangle. He did not wish to appear too eager for a familial reconciliation. "However, neither do I wish to see a connection of Catherine's hauled off to debtors' prison, a fate I understand awaits *you* in no short order."

Lady Carr's bosom swelled with rage and chagrin. Her face flushed an ugly red as she tried to contain her rage. Her only chance lay in the Barrington name and wealth. Barbara had whistled the marriage down the wind, but at least the chit Catherine had done something to earn her keep.

"What do you suggest?" she demanded with a snap. "I warn you I shall not retire gracefully to the country. I have no use for the life of a rustic. As well I have need of town connections, for I have two more girls to get off, as you well know."

"I had no notion to send you to the country," he retorted, a hard gleam in his eyes. "I wish you where I can see you."

Lady Carr goggled at the barely concealed menace. "What do you mean?"

"I mean that I know just the kind of woman you are. I have no desire to discover your tongue wagging in the country. Catherine has suffered enough at your hands. I want you here, and for that I am willing to pay. Pay well, mind, if you obey me. I shall see that your debts are covered provided they are rendered to my man of business and he pays directly to the source.''

"You do not trust me?"

"I thought I had made that clear." His lips twisted at her astounded expression. "Moreover, you will receive an allowance, but my man will also take over the running of your household. I place no great trust in your management to date." He ignored her hiss of outrage. "As for your offspring, I wish an accounting of their whereabouts and intentions. All of these are conditions for my bailing you out of the river tick. One mistake, and I withdraw my support.''

"This is monstrous! I will not allow you such licence!" She surged to her feet, glaring at him, then at Catherine. "You would let him do this to us, your own family?" Her voice was shrill.

Catherine felt a stirring of pity for the woman's plight, but she had not forgotten her treatment at her hands. "I think he is exceedingly generous," she said quietly, thinking how masterly Marcus's plan was. With one stroke he had negated the threat in which they stood and found a means to know Barbara's plans for the future. Lady Carr was mercenary enough to stick to the letter of the agreement, no matter the cost to her pride.

Lady Carr's hands clenched in very unladylike fists, her face a mottled red. She had come to get what was due her for all the years of housing Catherine. She had not counted on Marcus's standing against her. To her cost, she had believed Barbara when she said the marriage was not a real one.

"You leave me no choice, as you well know," she snapped furiously. "I suppose, too, that I must pretend to countenance this marriage and to have affection for you both?"

Marcus smiled at the sarcasm, genuinely amused for the first time since the interview began. "I do not think such drastic and, for us, distasteful measures are necessary. Courtesy will suffice, should we meet. And a still tongue in your head," he added on a hard note. "One rumour started by you or your daughter will bring consequences on your head which, I promise you, you will not like." He rose and moved to the door. Opening it, he gestured for her to leave. "I think we have done with our business."

Lady Carr stood for a long moment staring at him. All her plans were in ruins. Now she was dependent on him and on Catherine. The thought was galling. Damn Barbara and her infatuation with Lord March. But for her stupidity it would be she sitting beside Marcus and holding the purse strings.

"My lady," Marcus prompted firmly.

Her wrath needed an outlet, and it found one in Catherine. "You, miss, are an ungrateful wretch. I should have let you go to a home."

Marcus took a step toward Lady Carr, intending to defend Catherine. Catherine rose, her back straight, her eyes fixed on her aunt. Marcus had given her more than a home and caring. He had given her the security to speak her mind. "Had you done so it would have been a kindness, for I found none in your house. I was nothing more than an unpaid slave and well you know it. I came prepared to love you and my cousins, and all of you hated me." The words emerged without heat, a simple truth stated softly, more devastating for its quiet strength. Lady Carr stepped back, her eyes wide with shock. "I wish none of you ill, but I cannot but feel you have reaped precisely what you sowed. I can feel your hatred for me, but all I feel for you and yours is profound pity." Turning her face from her aunt's, she walked to Marcus's side, dismissing the woman from her mind. "I shall go and tend to luncheon." With a touch of her hand to his she left the room without a backward glance.

"As you can see," said Marcus, "there is no reason for you to stay longer."

Lady Carr looked into Marcus's eyes, finding no mercy in them. "She should hate me . . ."

He shook his head. "It is not in her to hate anyone."

Lady Carr swallowed hard, her rage dying in defeat. Slowly, beaten by Marcus's wealth and power and Catherine's quiet strength, she walked out the door.

"WHAT DID HE SAY, MOTHER?" Barbara demanded eagerly the moment Lady Carr entered the drawing room. "Did he come across with the ready?"

Lady Carr sank gratefully into a chair, her eyes fixed on Barbara's face. "He did, but not in any way that will do you any good, my girl. We are to render all our accounts to him with an allowance to me. Neither you, I, nor the girls may move without his knowledge, or we shall forfeit the whole."

Barbara paled. "He cannot mean it. It is all that spiteful Cat's fault."

Lady Carr sighed deeply, wearily. "I do not think it is. She is not the girl we thought."

"A few jewels," Barbara scoffed.

"More than that by far. You will see." She closed her eyes, no longer wishing to look upon her own child.

"I shall see nothing. I *shall* make them both wish they had not tried to control me."

"Then more fool you. Lord March has still not come up to scratch. Have you a mind to end your days in debtors' prison?"

"It will not come to that. Marcus will not allow it."

Lady Carr opened her eyes and glared at her daughter. "If you do or say one thing to cause either of them discomfort, I shall disown you," she stated clearly, meaning her threat with every ounce of her being. "You are bone selfish, miss, and do not think

I do not know it. But so am I. I make no apology for either of us, but even we should know when to quit. His lordship holds all the cards in this game. I have no wish to anger him further. Add to that, your precious Lord March will have little to say to you should you end up in such a place. Your beauty will not save you from prison, nor would it withstand the life."

Barbara matched her parent stare for stare for a moment, then she subsided into sullen silence as she realized the rightness of her words.

"Better you should apply yourself to bringing his lordship to the point. You, at least, will be out of this." She closed her eyes again and waved her hand toward the door. "Now go away and let me rest. I have had enough of our problems for now."

# CHAPTER TWELVE

"Do you truly think it will serve, Marcus?" Catherine asked.

Marcus sat on the sofa and drew Catherine down so that she sat in his lap. Wrapping his arms around her, he leaned his cheek against her hair. The house was quiet, the servants dismissed, and it was just the two of them alone. He had never known being with a woman and simply talking could hold such quiet delight.

"Sir John thought it a master stroke when I spoke to him this afternoon. He has assigned a man to watch your aunt's house. He has also had word that a ship has docked in Dover which is bound to leave for France two nights from now. The man who brought him the information said the captain is prepared to receive an august personage on board, perhaps with a lady. Sir John cannot be sure, but he thinks Lord March is the personage."

"And Barbara the lady? I cannot believe she will do such a thing." Catherine snuggled close, savouring the warmth of his arms about her. Held safe against him, she knew a contentment too deep for mere words.

"That is one of the reasons I made my conditions so unbearable. Barbara has pride. If anything can drive her to this it will be living on a stipend from us."

Catherine lifted her head from his chest. "You wish her to go with Robert?"

"I wish her away where she cannot hurt you. If she stays in London, then you will be forever in her way. She is not kind."

"You mean to let Robert go?"

"If possible. His death will serve no one. The memo is what matters, and once his activities are known he will not dare to show his face in London again."

"I had not realized others would know of his perfidy."

"Better this way than death." Marcus frowned a little. "Were I in his shoes I do not know what I should do. A man of two countries, ties and families in both. How does one choose a path with divided loyalties?"

"I had not thought of that."

Lightly stroking the furrow between her brows, he smiled at her earnest expression. "A terrible oversight on your part, my Kate."

She playfully nipped at the finger he brushed across her lips. "You shall not tease me, my lord." The flicker of desire in his eyes pleased her greatly.

If only one day he would speak of love, her world would be complete.

"I shall not, madam wife? What would you prefer I do?"

"Many things, all of which you know, but first, tell me the rest of the plan."

Recognizing the stubborn expression on her face, he sighed deeply. "For such a sweet-natured woman, you can be amazingly mulish on occasion." He kissed her hard, urgently. "I would talk later," he whispered. On feeling her *no* pass from her lips to his, he lifted his head, glaring at her for putting his passion off. He wanted her now, not later.

Catherine smiled softly and stroked his cheek. "Now who is being mulish?"

"My lady, you are becoming a bit too knowing," he muttered, glaring more when she laughed. "And I too soft. I can see I must change my ways."

"You are digressing."

He was, but he had hoped she would not notice. "You will not like it."

"There is very little here that I do like. I wish to get on with our life, not ferret out spies in my own family," she pointed out tartly.

"Touché, my love." He settled her closer to his heart and tucked her head under his chin. "If I must do this then I wish to be comfortable." He took a moment to gather his thoughts. "The plan is simple. The man watching your aunt's house will report to Sir John and to us the moment Barbara makes a move to join Lord March. You and I shall take a freakish idea into our heads to travel to my estate near Dover." He ignored her small start of surprise. "I shall confront his lordship and threaten him with a public trial for treason, offering him at the same time a chance to leave the country minus the memo, with only the rumours of his crimes to stain his time here. We are hoping he will choose the latter, but there will be men with us to take him prisoner should he not do so."

"And Barbara?"

"That is why you will be with me. Should she choose not to accompany Robert to France then we shall lend her countenance by saying that she had need of a rest and that we had taken her down with us to the country. There will be gossip, of course, but her reputation will not be ruined beyond repair. Then I shall set about finding her a country squire to wed."

"It will serve, I suppose," Catherine murmured after a moment. "But she will hate either course."

Marcus's smile, which Catherine did not see, was not nice. "The die was cast long before now," he reminded her gently, before turning her in his arms. "Now, wife, let us think of us. We can rest easy until our man reports."

Catherine melted against him, easily caught in the love filling her heart. "As always, I am at your command, my lord."

Marcus laughed aloud, hugging her. "That is a blatant lie, madam. I am the most henpecked of husbands.'' He rose with her in his arms. Her fragile weight made no impression on his wound. For her he was strong. He glanced down at her, smiling. Her smile was a match and a challenge as he strode from the room, holding her like a precious treasure in his arms.

THE DARKNESS WAS BROKEN by the glow of the street lamp. The man watching the Carr house stood hidden in the shadows. A four-in-hand eased slowly down the street, stopping near the corner. A passenger alighted and strode quickly to the back of the house. Lord March. It was time, the trap was sprung. Signalling his partner to keep watch the man hurried from his post. His first stop was the Barrington residence.

THE THUNDEROUS KNOCKING at the front door penetrated Marcus's sleep. Groaning, he stumbled from bed and pulled on his robe. Catherine opened her eyes, no less alert than he.

"Is it time?"

"It would seem so. Dress as quickly as you can," he bade, striding from the room.

Catherine jumped from the bed and hurried to her dressing room. A dark gown, something warm. In a trice she was ready. She returned to the master suite as Marcus entered from his own dressing room, attired from head to toe in unrelieved black. His face was harsh in the muted lights of the candles. Holding out her hand to him, she said, "I had hoped that he would not do this, and that it would not be Lord March."

"There is no mistake. The man recognized him and his matched team of blacks. It is well that my bays are up to snuff, otherwise we would be hard pressed to keep up. As it is, we must make haste." He took Catherine's cloak and tossed it about her shoulders. "You left the note for Mary Rose to follow us to Dover tomorrow?"

"And one for the housekeeper, as you suggested," she agreed as they moved quickly down the stairs. "You know we shall seem a flighty pair."

Marcus grinned at the thought. "There are worse things to be thought." He sobered quickly. "A spy for one." They gained the front door just as their lightly sprung carriage rolled into view. Bates rode beside the coachman, his wizened figure swathed in an overcoat. "I thought I told you to stay," Marcus muttered, directing a mild glare at his valet.

"You may have need of me, and I am not needed here," Bates returned.

Had Marcus the time he would have argued the point, a fact of which he knew Bates was fully aware. "One day I shall remember that I have the power to pension you off," he threatened, ignoring Bates's grin.

Catherine smiled at the exchange, amazed she could find anything amusing this night. Marcus handed her into the coach, barely settling himself before the horses were away. The streets were nearly deserted, making their passage swift and sure. Neither spoke for the first few miles.

"If you can, sleep, my Kate. The journey is tedious."

Catherine looked at him as he leaned comfortably in the corner of the coach. He seemed at home with the night and the errand of national import. She knew she was seeing a facet of him which few women were privileged to know of their husbands. "I do not think I could sleep," she admitted.

"There is no woman I can think of that I would take with me this night," he said quietly. "You do not hold a man up with useless questions or missish female dawdlings. Had I known of another way to save Barbara's reputation I would not have exposed you to this journey." He rose and moved to join her. "If you are worried, I can have Bates conduct you to our estate. I shall bring Barbara to you there, if she comes."

"No, I would stay with you. I am glad you need me. I would wish always to be at your side."

"You are sure? This could be dangerous."

"I have you to protect me."

His eyes held hers, reading the absolute faith and trust in them. For all the days of his life he would bless the impulse which had prompted him to ask for her hand in marriage. And it was in that moment he knew that he loved her. Had they the time he would have gone on his knees before her and confessed his heart. But their needs must wait for the greater good.

"With my life, my lady." He pulled her into his arms and settled her head on his shoulder. "But for now, try to rest. The night will be long."

Catherine closed her eyes, inhaling his scent and feeling safe. He wished her to rest, so she would.

"CATHERINE, AWAKE. We have arrived," Marcus whispered as the lights of the inn at Dover came into view.

Catherine stirred, realizing that she had indeed fallen asleep. "I am not much of a companion I fear," she murmured, missing the warmth of his arms as he released her. She carefully straightened her clothes and replaced her bonnet atop the smooth braid of hair.

Marcus jumped down as soon as the coach pulled to a stop. "Tom, see to Lord March's coach. We do not wish him to leave without our knowing. Bates, secure us a chamber where her ladyship may rest." The men hopped to the tasks set them with a will. Marcus turned to hand Catherine down. "Now for our part," he said, guiding her across the cobbled courtyard.

The inn was small but scrupulously clean. At this time of night it was also quiet, as most travellers were abed. Candles burned in the hall sockets and a lamp on the desk where the visitors could sign or mark in. The innkeeper, an individual as round as he was tall, came out of the back room, his eyes widening on seeing yet another pair of Quality.

"Cor, an' there be much doin' on this road this night," he muttered, ambling toward them. "You be wantin' a chamber?"

"My man will see to it," Marcus said, glancing around. As far as he could see there was none around to lend aid to Lord March should he make a fight of it. Marcus did not think it likely with the ladies present, but he wanted nothing to endanger Catherine or his mission.

"I believe some friends of ours are here. We are to meet and travel on the morrow together."

The innkeeper glanced at his best parlour. "Aye, if you be meanin' the pretty lady and her gent, they be there in my best room. Awaitin' a ship they are. You be goin' to that Frenchie nest with 'em?"

Marcus ignored the question as he urged Catherine down the narrow passage to the closed door at the end. "Are you ready, my dear?"

"As ever," she said softly, not about to add to his trouble by admitting her fear. Marcus might think her brave, but she was not, not as he. Any courage she'd shown had come of circumstances. This was choice. For him she would stand, but for herself she would have preferred not.

For an instant, Marcus's eyes reflected his pride, then he pushed open the door. The pair seated before the fire froze at the interruption. Catherine studied her cousin, surprised at the pity she felt for her. The love shining on the beautiful face was plain for all to see.

"Barrington." Lord March rose, his dark brows conveying his shock at seeing them. "It would seem you have a whim to travel as we."

"The difference being that we are married," Marcus returned bluntly.

"As we soon shall be," Lord March replied just as smartly.

"Without consent of her family."

"It will not matter in this case. I have decided to return to my homeland. The Lady Barbara makes the journey with me as my bride. We are to be married on board ship."

Marcus glanced at Barbara. "Is that your wish?"

"It is, although I know not what business it is of yours," she snapped.

"Rest easy, my pet." Lord March laid a hand on Barbara's shoulder, his fingers holding her in place when she would have jumped to her feet in temper.

"Then I and my wife shall wish you a safe journey, provided you return something you have which does not belong to you." Marcus faced his adversary, his eyes hard and without mercy.

Robert stilled, his faint air of amusement dying at Marcus's words. "I do not know what you mean."

"I can be more enlightening if you wish." His glance travelled to Barbara and back again.

Lord March's eyes narrowed. His hand slipped to the small pistol he carried concealed on his person.

"That will not be necessary. Nor will I return what you seek. I cannot. It is of more value to me than you can imagine."

Marcus moved to stand in front of Catherine. Danger was in the room. He would not have her hurt. "Hand it over, and you and Lady Barbara go free. Otherwise I will take you back to London to stand trial for treason. Your family will suffer on both sides of the channel. You cannot want that."

"Treason? What treason? Robert?" Barbara came to her feet, amazement written on her face. She tugged at Lord March's sleeve. "He is lying, is he not?" she demanded.

"He is not," Robert answered without taking his eyes from Marcus. "I am not the only one who will suffer," he murmured.

"For myself I have no reason to care. For Catherine and her connection I do, but it would not stop me from doing what must be done. Your choice."

Barbara turned on Marcus, angry, confused and frightened at feeling her future slip away yet again. "I will not not have it, do you hear me?" She grabbed up the teapot sitting on the table and before anyone could stop her hurled it at Marcus's head.

Catherine gasped and tried to throw herself in front of the missile. Marcus dodged. Barbara's skirts tangled in Robert's legs as he drew his pistol, throwing him off balance. The weapon slipped from his fingers, falling on the table before Barbara. Snatching it up, she pointed it at Catherine, the closest target.

"I shall fire," she shrieked, beyond thinking. Her hand shook as she levelled the gun.

Catherine froze, knowing her cousin in a temper was likely to do anything.

"Don't be a fool, Barbara. You will not escape. There are men outside. You will be stopped," Marcus pointed out, speaking as calmly as he was able.

Robert fingered the memo in his pocket. Murder had never been in his plans, but he did not intend to lose his birthright. "Hold, my pet. He is right." He pulled the paper from his coat and tossed it on the table. "We cannot escape."

Barbara swung round. Marcus jumped for the memo and at the same time bumped Catherine out of the way. Robert pulled the gun from Barbara's hand and levelled it on Marcus. "Give it to me," he commanded, his expression revealing that for him there was no going back.

Marcus reluctantly handed the paper over. Robert glanced at it, then pulled Barbara close. "Make your choice, my lady. Stay or go?"

Barbara glared at Marcus and Catherine. "There is nothing I wish for here. Let us leave this place forever."

Robert nodded once and picked up his cloak without lowering the pistol. "So be it. Let us be gone." He headed for the door, leaving Barbara to collect her own cloak and follow. "You will understand that I shall lock you in and pay the innkeeper well to keep you that way until the ship sails on the tide. Less than an hour.'' He smiled a little as he set his hat upon his head. ''You have honour, my friend, and courage. I could have liked you.'' He ushered Barbara through the door, slamming and locking it behind him.

Catherine stared at the panel, then turned to Marcus. ''Bates will miss us soon. We can still catch Lord March.''

Marcus shook his head. ''Bates has orders to look the other way.''

Catherine frowned at the odd pronouncement. ''But why? He will escape with the memo.''

''As I hoped.'' Marcus sat down in the chair which Robert recently vacated. ''If I learned one thing on the battlefield it was to prepare for the unexpected. I had hoped that with you and Barbara here he would give up gracefully. I did not think it, however, given the stakes. So Sir John and I concocted a fake memo. I exchanged it with the real one in the scuffle. I have the real memo.''

''You let him escape? You planned for this.'' Without thinking, Catherine took the chair beside him and the small glass of wine he poured for her.

''It seemed the best course for us all. Barbara will be well away, in exile from her home, perhaps, but with a man who will not let her run free. Your aunt will have no ally to harm you, and England will be rid of one who would sell his soul for a few acres of French land."

"You did not tell me."

"I was not sure it would work."

Catherine pondered that. "I believe you knew it would."

Marcus said nothing.

"Do we sit now until Bates comes?"

"If you wish. But more than that I wish to plan a trip away for just the two of us."

Catherine stared at him, taken aback at the suggestion. "What kind of trip?"

"A wedding trip."

The warm look in his eyes was eloquent. Catherine took a hasty sip of her wine, feeling the heat of the liquid slip down her throat. Her dream shone before her, but this time she was almost afraid to believe it was within her grasp. "But why?"

"I have a need to be alone with my wife. To show her how much she means to me . . . how very much I love her. To tell her how glad I am that I asked her to be my wife. To speak of children and growing old and the things we shall do. To hold her in my arms and watch the sunset. To sleep with her beside me until the sun rises." He took the glass from her hand and set it on the table. "Do you suppose she would like that?"

"I think she would like that very well indeed," she assured him, going into his arms.

Marcus held her tight, feeling her softness yield to his strength. "I love you, my Catherine. I did not look for love, had believed it dead within me, but you showed me my belief was not so."

Catherine touched his cheek, her fingers tracing his scar. "I prayed each night for this. I loved you so much."

Marcus stared into her eyes and knew he would never be able to tell her how important she was to him. He could only show her, living with her day by day. Sharing his life, his thoughts and his love. Marcus kissed her then, knowing the future held more than he dreamed. His misfit wife was perfect for him in every way. She was his complement, his mate, his love. She had shown him the courage of facing an imperfect world and making it whole. She had led him out of the darkness of his despair with her love, and he would spend his days loving and keeping her safe from those who would see her gentleness and kind heart as weakness. Together they would build a life and raise children born of their love.

# *Harlequin Regency Romance*™

---

## COMING NEXT MONTH

**#15 THE VIRGIN'S HEART by Coral Hoyle**
Amidst the backdrop of country courting and
competition, Alexander Monk is determined to win
back Roxanne Costain, the woman who had ended
their betrothal four years before. A treasure hunt,
conceived to make them "partners," begins as a romp
but ends in treachery and near tragedy for Roxanne
and Alex. The brush with disaster seals their love and
they pledge anew their vows to wed.

**#16 MEN WERE DECEIVERS EVER by Gwyneth Moore**
When Helena Hammond learns her fiancé was killed
in the war, she accepts the proposal of marriage made
by Lt. Peter Clivedon. Her family is deeply in debt—
she sees no alternative. Once married and removed to
Whisperwood, Helena grows very fond of Peter. But
the idyllic interlude is shattered when Helena learns
Peter tricked and deceived her into marriage. Though
she leaves Whisperwood vowing never to come back,
Peter can only hope she never finds out the
devastating truth behind his proposal.

# Montana Man

## BARBARA DELINSKY

When you think of Harlequin Temptation, it's hard not to
think of Barbara Delinsky. She was there from the start to
help establish Temptation as a fresh, exciting line featur-
ing extremely talented storytellers. The title of her very
first Temptation—*A Special Something*—describes what
Barbara has continued to bring to you over the years.

We thought it was high time to officially recognize Barbara Delinsky's contribution to Harlequin. And by happy
coincidence, she gave us *Montana Man* for publication in
December. We couldn't have hoped for a better book to
carry Harlequin's Award of Excellence or a better gift to
give *you* during the holiday season.

It's tempting to say that, of Barbara's eighteen Temp-
tations, *Montana Man* is the most moving, most satisfy-
ing, most wonderful story she's ever written. But each of
her books evokes that response. We'll let you be the judge
in December....

AE-MM-1

# Especially for you,
# Christmas from
# HARLEQUIN HISTORICALS

An enchanting collection of three Christmas
stories by some of your favorite authors captures
the spirit of the season in the 1800s

## TUMBLEWEED CHRISTMAS by Kristin James

A "Bah, humbug" Texas rancher meets his match in his
new housekeeper, a woman determined to bring the spirit
of a Tumbleweed Christmas into his life—and love into
his heart.

## A CINDERELLA CHRISTMAS by Lucy Elliot

The perfect granddaughter, sister and aunt, Mary Hillyer
seemed destined for spinsterhood until Jack Gates arrived
to discover a woman with dreams and passions that were
meant to be shared during a Cinderella Christmas.

## HOME FOR CHRISTMAS
## by Heather Graham Pozzessere

The magic of the season brings peace Home For
Christmas when a Yankee captain and a Southern heiress
fall in love during the Civil War.

Look for HARLEQUIN HISTORICALS CHRISTMAS
STORIES in November wherever Harlequin books are sold.

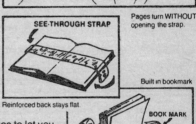

# HARLEQUIN'S "BIG WIN"
## SWEEPSTAKES RULES & REGULATIONS
### NO PURCHASE NECESSARY TO ENTER OR RECEIVE A PRIZE

1. To enter and join the Harlequin Reader Service, scratch off the pink metallic strips on all your BIG WIN tickets #1-#6. This will reveal the values for each sweepstakes entry number, the number of free books you will receive and your free bonus gift as part of our Reader Service. If you do not wish to take advantage of our introduction to the Harlequin Reader Service but wish to enter the Sweepstakes only, scratch off the pink metallic strips on your BIG WIN tickets #1-#4 only. To enter, return your entire sheet of tickets intact. Incomplete and/or inaccurate entries are not eligible for that section or section(s) of prizes. Not responsible for mutilated or unreadable entries or inadvertent printing errors. Mechanically reproduced entries are null and void. Be sure to also qualify for the Bonus Sweepstakes. See Rule #3 on how to enter.

2. Either way your unique Sweepstakes numbers will be compared against the list of winning numbers generated at random by the computer. In the event that all prizes are not claimed, random drawings will be held from all entries received from all presentations to award all unclaimed prizes. All cash prizes are payable in U.S. funds. This is in addition to any free, surprise or mystery gifts that might be offered. The following prizes are awarded in this sweepstakes: *Grand Prize (1) $1,000,000; First Prize (1) $35,000; Second Prize (1) $10,000; Third Prize (3) $5,000; Fourth Prize (10) $1,000; Fifth Prize (25) $500; Sixth Prize (5000) $5.

   *This Sweepstakes contains a Grand Prize offering of a $1,000,000 annuity. Winner may elect to receive $25,000 a year for 40 years without interest totalling $1,000,000 or $350,000 in one cash payment. Entrants may cancel Reader Service at any time without cost or obligation to buy (see details in center insert card).

3. Extra Bonus Prize: This presentation offers two extra bonus prizes valued at $30,000 each to be awarded in a random drawing from all entries received.

4. Versions of this Sweepstakes with different graphics will be offered in other mailings or at retail outlets by Torstar Corp. and its affiliates. This promotion is being conducted under the supervision of Marden-Kane, Inc., an independent judging organization. By entering this Sweepstakes, each entrant accepts and agrees to be bound by these rules and the decisions of the judges, which shall be final and binding. Odds of winning in the random drawing are dependent upon the total number of entries received. Taxes, if any, are the sole responsibility of the winners. Prizes are non-transferable. All entries must be received by March 31, 1990. The drawing will take place on or about April 30, 1990 at the offices of Marden-Kane, Inc., Lake Success, NY.

5. This offer is open to residents of the U.S., the United Kingdom and Canada, 18 years or older except employees of Torstar Corp., its affiliates, subsidiaries, Marden-Kane, Inc. and all other agencies and persons connected with conducting this Sweepstakes. All Federal, State and local laws apply. Void wherever prohibited or restricted by law.

6. Winners will be notified by mail and may be required to execute an affidavit of eligibility and release that must be returned within 14 days after notification. Canadian winners will be required to answer a skill-testing question. Winners consent to the use of their name, photograph and/or likeness for advertising and publicity in conjunction with this and similar promotions without additional compensation.

7. For a list of our most current major prize winners, send a stamped, self-addressed envelope to: WINNERS LIST c/o MARDEN-KANE, INC., P.O. BOX 701, SAYREVILLE, NJ 08871.

---

If Sweepstakes entry form is missing, please print your name and address on a 3" x 5" piece of plain paper and send to:

In the U.S.
Harlequin "BIG WIN" Sweepstakes
901 Fuhrmann Blvd.
Box 1867
Buffalo, NY 14269-1867

In Canada
Harlequin "BIG WIN" Sweepstakes
P.O. Box 609
Fort Erie, Ontario
L2A 5X3

LTY-H119

Wonderful, luxurious gifts can be yours with proofs-of-purchase from any specially marked "Indulge A Little" Harlequin or Silhouette book with the Offer Certificate properly completed, plus a check or money order (do not send cash) to cover postage and handling payable to Harlequin/Silhouette "Indulge A Little, Give A Lot" Offer. We will send you the specified gift.

**Mail-in-Offer**

**OFFER CERTIFICATE**

| Item: | A. Collector's Doll | B. Soaps in a Basket | C. Potpourri Sachet | D. Scented Hangers |
|---|---|---|---|---|
| # of Proofs-of -Purchase | 18 | 12 | 6 | 4 |
| Postage & Handling | $3.25 | $2.75 | $2.25 | $2.00 |
| Check One | | | | |

Name _____

Address _____ Apt. # _____

City _____ State _____ Zip _____

**ONE PROOF OF PURCHASE**

To collect your free gift by mail you must include the necessary number of proofs-of-purchase plus postage and handling with offer certificate.

HRG-2

Harlequin®/Silhouette®

Mail this certificate, designated number of proofs-of-purchase and check or money order for postage and handling to:

**INDULGE A LITTLE**
**P.O. Box 9055**
**Buffalo, N.Y. 14269-9055**